pugs
and
kisses

Also by J.J. Howard

Sit, Stay, Love

pugs
and
kisses

j.j. howard

SCHOLASTIC INC.

Copyright © 2018 by Jennifer Howard

All rights reserved. Published by Scholastic Inc., *Publishers since 1920.* SCHOLASTIC and associated logos are trademarks and/or registered trademarks of Scholastic Inc.

The publisher does not have any control over and does not assume any responsibility for author or third-party websites or their content.

ISBN 978-1-338-19457-9

10 9 8 7 6 5 4 3 2 1   18 19 20 21 22

Printed in the U.S.A.   40
First printing 2018

Book design by Yaffa Jaskoll

For Aimee.
Thanks for believing, starting way
back in our circus days.

pugs
and
kisses

1

Noah's Ark Theory

I know it's weird to wake up early on a Saturday, but this wasn't just any Saturday; it was my birthday. And once I opened my eyes, I was totally awake.

I sat up in bed and thought: *This* could be the year when my wish for a dog of my own could come true. Because I had more than just a wish—I had a plan.

In our family, we have two birthday traditions: one, the breakfast cupcake, and two, you get to pick one place you want to go. This year, I wasn't picking a restaurant or a movie or a store. My place was going to be the dog shelter on Avenue B. I'd checked the other day, and they had tons of puppies. I hadn't let myself look *too* closely at any of them—I didn't want to accidentally fall in love with one of their cute, furry faces, just in case my plan didn't work out.

I got out of bed quietly, so as not to wake up my older sister, Talisa, who was asleep in her bed across our room. I went into the bathroom to wash up, and as I peered at my reflection in the mirror, I wondered if I looked any different now that I was a year older. But I had to admit that I looked pretty much the same: shoulder-length wavy brown hair; brown skin; light brown eyes . . . and still very short. I hadn't had a birthday growth spurt overnight, that was for sure.

I returned to my room and got dressed in the semi-dark, thinking about the next part of my plan. Even though Mom had been saying "no dogs allowed" for as long as I'd been alive, I had science on my side. Or at least, a theory of my grandmother's. When my sister and I were little, Abuelita Elena used to tell us about her "Noah's Ark theory." She said that, just like the animals on the ark, everything works better in pairs.

Now, I don't have a dog of my own, but I do help take care of a dog almost every day. Osito is an adorable black pug that belongs to my upstairs neighbor Mrs. Ramirez. Mrs. R is in her sixties, and she had to have surgery on her back last year, so she has trouble with the stairs in our building. I help her out by walking Osito and taking him to the dog run in the park for some exercise. But Osito's been kind of down lately. He and I are very close, so I can tell. I think he needs to be part of a pair. If *I* had a dog for him to hang out with in the building he wouldn't be alone anymore. Both Osito and Mrs. R would be happier. And me, too, of course.

The problem is, Mom's not the hugest fan of my spending so much time with Osito. But she never says I can't take him out, because she knows Mrs. R needs the help.

I tied my sneakers, glanced at the time, and decided I'd have a quick bowl of cereal before heading upstairs to get Osito for his walk. Then I remembered—no boring old cereal today! There was a delicious cupcake from Butter Lane waiting for me in the kitchen. Mom always left the birthday cupcake sitting at your place at the table. I dashed out of my room, went straight to the kitchen and over to my spot at the table, and saw . . . no cupcake.

Instead, there was a note from Mom. And not a happy-birthday note, either.

Hi, Ana! When you have a chance, can you please go to Mr. Levy's store and pick up the piñata for Talisa's quinceañera?
Thanks!
Love,
Mami

I felt all the excitement whoosh right out of me. Had Mom forgotten my cupcake? Or worse, had she been so busy preparing for Tali's future birthday that she'd completely forgotten *mine*? What if *everyone* had forgotten? Things had been pretty crazy around here, with everyone getting ready for the huge party to celebrate Tali's fifteenth birthday. And yes, a *quinceañera* was a big deal . . . but still.

I stood in the silent kitchen for a moment, feeling lonesome. I knew that Mom was still sleeping, and my dad had left already; he works at a bank and sometimes has to go in on Saturdays. With a sigh, I grabbed Mom's note and balled it up, shoving it into the pocket of my jacket. Suddenly I felt like getting out of the apartment as fast as possible. I poured some dry cereal into a plastic baggie and decided I'd eat my non-special breakfast in the park. So far this birthday wasn't off to a great start.

I walked upstairs to Mrs. Ramirez's apartment and knocked on the door.

"Hi, Ana—come on in—you can use your key!" Mrs. R called.

As soon as I pushed open the door, Osito sprang up from where he'd been lying on the floor. He barreled toward me at top speed, jumping up on his short legs to try to greet me. I knelt down and giggled as he licked my face. When he settled down a tiny bit—just enough to stop licking me—I kissed the top of his head and rubbed his little ears. His short fur felt soft and silky to the touch. His round black eyes gazed up at me in adoration and I couldn't help cooing at him that he was such a good boy.

Osito gave a happy puppy sigh, then flopped back down on the floor.

"*Hola*, Ana," Mrs. R said from where she was lying on the couch. "He's been moping all morning. I'm glad you're here to take him out for some fresh air."

I nodded, getting to my feet and grabbing Osito's harness off the wall hook. The pug got back up and his tail wagged. He didn't seem as energetic as usual, though. I remembered when I first started walking him and every time I reached for the harness, he'd do a happy dance. This dog definitely needed a friend.

"I'll take him to the park, and I also need to go by Mr. Levy's for my mom," I said. "Do you want me to bring you anything?"

"No, I'm fine, *mija*. Thank you. I don't know what I'd do without you."

"I don't mind at all. I love spending time with the little guy."

"Oh, Ana?" Mrs. R said just as I was opening the door, Osito at my heels. "Isn't today your birthday? Happy birthday!"

"Thanks, Mrs. R," I said, smiling back at her. At least *some-one* remembered!

Osito and I headed downstairs and outside. The morning air

was chilly, but it felt good after the stuffiness of Mrs. R's apartment. She'd said that she was feeling fine, but it seemed to me that she was a lot more subdued than when I'd first known her, too. Maybe Osito was picking up on his owner's feelings, and that was why he seemed a little blue.

I stopped in to Mr. Levy's shop on the way to the park and picked up the piñata Mom had ordered. With that errand taken care of, my spirits began to lift, and so did Osito's. We entered the park, and Osito barked happily as we approached the enclosed dog run area. I smiled. It was a crisp, bright day, and I was determined to shake off my disappointment from the morning. Nothing could bring me down!

And then, as if the universe had heard my thoughts, it suddenly started to rain.

2

A Pug Named Pancake

It wasn't just any sort of a rain, but a real downpour. Osito and I were already in the dog run, but everyone else around us—dogs and owners—began to scatter like leaves in the wind. I didn't know where to run off to; the storm was right on top of us.

The wind whipped my hair out of its ponytail holder. My hair flapped in front of my face, making it hard to see. The rain pelted against my skin; my clothes were already half soaked. On top of all that, I was wrestling with the giant shopping bag that contained the piñata.

Things went from bad to worse as Osito spotted another dog and took off running toward it. His soaking-wet leash slipped right through my fingers. All I could see of the other dog was a flash of tan fur. I yelled for Osito to come back, but the wind seemed to steal my voice away.

I saw another shape coming toward me and realized it must be the other dog's owner. As the figure got closer I saw it was a boy who looked to be about the same age as me.

The boy reached out for his tan-colored dog, but it slipped out of his grasp and headed straight for Osito. The two dogs sniffed each other's rears in classic dog fashion, and then Osito rolled onto his back and the other dog jumped on him. They rolled around happily like two puppies. I gasped when I realized that the other dog was also a pug.

The two pugs kept rolling around, tiny tails wagging a mile a minute, as though it weren't pouring rain and thundering all around them.

The boy looked at me helplessly and then he reached into his pocket and pulled out a baggie.

"Treats!" he yelled over a clap of thunder. He took a few biscuits out of the bag and stepped in closer to the dogs. His pug recognized the smell and stopped playing. The boy grabbed his dog, and I went for Osito. I wasn't taking any chances with the wet leash this time—I grabbed the whole dog.

"I see a roof over there!" the boy yelled. "Make a run for it?" He pointed to the pavilion outside the dog run.

I nodded. "Let's go."

I started forward, then realized I'd forgotten my shopping bag. As I tried to figure out how to pick up the bag without putting Osito down, the boy shifted his dog to one arm and grabbed the bag for me. I gave him a grateful smile, and then we were both running toward the pavilion.

We ducked under the roof, then collapsed onto a bench at one of the picnic tables. It felt good to get out of the pounding rain. I wrapped the end of Osito's leash around my hand a couple of times, then put the pug down on the ground. I gathered up my wet hair with my free hand and pulled down, slicking out the water like I would if I'd just climbed out of a swimming pool.

At our feet, Osito and the light brown pug, each on their leashes, started to play again.

I heard the boy beside me chuckle. "Weird," he said, nodding toward his dog. "I haven't seen her like this in a while." He looked over at me. "That's Pancake, by the way."

"Her new best friend's name is Osito. And I'm Ana."

"Calvin," the boy said, with a slightly shy smile. "Osito—that's a cool name."

"It means *little bear*," I told him. "In Spanish."

Now that we were out of the rain I could see the boy, Calvin, clearly. For one thing, I could see that he was very cute. He was white, with brown hair and hazel eyes that looked almost gold. He was also tall, taller than most boys my age. And he was clearly also very chivalrous for a boy my age, considering how he'd grabbed my bag for me. Most of the boys at my school seemed content to walk ahead of you through a door and let it slam in your face.

I realized I'd probably been staring at Calvin too long and looked away quickly.

"It's funny that we both have pugs," he said.

"Funny," I echoed.

"He does kind of look like a little black bear," Calvin said.

"Yep. And Pancake is a perfect pug name," I told him. "With their flat faces. Plus she's pancake-colored."

"Yeah, I thought the same thing about her color. Pugs are the best, aren't they?" Calvin asked with a smile.

And the award for the cutest boy I've met so far in life—who loves pugs as much as I do—definitely goes to Calvin.

I nodded, blushing.

"Hey, the rain's almost stopped," Calvin said. "I can't believe that storm's over so quickly."

"It must have been a single-cell thunderstorm," I said without thinking.

Then I held my breath. Now I'd find out if Calvin was the sort of boy who minded when my know-it-all side came out. Most kids my age didn't care about the science part of storms.

"Good thing it wasn't a derecho thunderstorm," Calvin agreed without missing a beat. "We could've been trapped under here for days."

A cute boy who didn't mind when I rattled off storm facts? In fact, he'd shared one of his own? Okay, he hadn't pronounced *derecho* exactly right, but I didn't even feel the urge to correct him.

Maybe it was too bad it *hadn't* been a derecho thunderstorm. Right at that moment I wouldn't mind being stuck there with Calvin for an entire day.

But then my cell phone buzzed in my pocket. I pulled it out to see a bunch of texts from my mom, asking where I was. I hadn't realized how much time had passed.

"I should get going," I told Calvin reluctantly. We stood up from the bench and Calvin picked up my shopping bag again. I couldn't help but smile as Osito and I followed Calvin and Pancake out of the park.

On the sidewalk, Osito and Pancake started smelling each other once more, still wagging their short curly tails.

"Fast friends," Calvin observed, and for a few seconds I thought maybe he meant us.

"Do you come to this park often?" I asked. I hadn't seen Calvin—or Pancake—there before, but didn't want to admit that. I was trying to act casual.

"Today was the first time, actually," Calvin said. "My family just moved to New York City. To this neighborhood. But I know Pancake and I will be back. How about you and Osito?"

"We come all the time," I said, bending down to scratch Osito behind the ears. I felt my phone buzz in my pocket again. Mom, for sure. "I have to go home now. Thank you for carrying my bag."

"Which way are you headed?"

I pointed east toward Avenue C. "That way."

Calvin looked around for a second; he seemed to be orienting himself. "I think I'm over that way? Ninth Street—off of First Avenue?"

I nodded. "Yep, you're the other way. Okay, well, hopefully we'll see you—and Pancake—soon!" I told him.

He smiled and handed me my bag back. "Nice to meet you, Ana from Avenue C."

"You, too, Calvin from Ninth Street," I said.

I watched him turn and head west. Then I started double-timing it back home.

"Come on, little bear," I urged Osito, and he did pick up the pace, moving quickly on his small paws. His tail wagged again, and I smiled at the memory of him and Pancake playing together.

Suddenly, it hit me—during my talk with Calvin, I'd never said that Osito wasn't technically my dog, that he belonged to my upstairs neighbor. Oh well. I figured I'd set Calvin straight when we ran into each other again.

Or, rather, *if* we did. New York was a big city, and there were lots of boys, and lots of dogs.

3

Paper Mache Is Not Waterproof

I dropped Osito off with Mrs. R, and then dashed back downstairs and into my apartment. I walked into the kitchen and took in the scene of chaos: Bags and boxes were everywhere. It seemed Mom was having one of her control-freak sessions, when she took inventory of all the items she was stockpiling for Talisa's *quinceañera*.

In the middle of the mess stood my sister, drowning in a frothy pink dress that had to be at least two sizes too big.

"What happened to you?" I asked her.

Before my sister could answer, Mom appeared, and looked

at me in horror. "What happened to *you*? You're making a puddle!"

"I got caught in the storm," I said. I put the wet bag down on the floor and shrugged out of my soaked jacket.

Mom *tsk*'ed and shook her head. She took my jacket and walked it to the sink, just as Talisa started singing.

"Happy birthday to you," Tali trilled in her pretty voice, "happy birthday to you, happy birthday, dear Ana . . ."

Mom let out a gasp and put a hand to her mouth. A look of horror crossed her face. *Aha.* So she *had* forgotten my birthday. My stomach sank.

"I'm sorry, *mija*!" Mom cried, putting the jacket aside and running over to me. "Happy birthday!" She cupped my chin in her hands, frowning, and then kissed my forehead. It made me feel only marginally better. "The cupcake!" she continued, looking guilty. "I meant to set it out last night but it slipped my mind." She turned to open the fridge and began rooting around inside. "And then this morning I knew you'd be leaving early to walk Osito, and Tali's dress was delivered, and it does *not* fit, as you can see . . ."

"I thought you forgot to get the cupcake," I said glumly, hearing the whine in my own voice.

Mom finally found what she was looking for in the fridge and came back to stand in front of me. She held out a Butter Lane crème brûlée cupcake—my favorite—with a candle in it. "See? I wouldn't forget tradition."

"Thanks, Mami," I said, taking the cupcake from her. My stomach growled. What with the rain and Calvin and Pancake, I hadn't had a chance to eat the dry cereal I'd packed for breakfast. Maybe now I could enjoy my birthday cupcake in peace, and . . .

"You're still dripping," Mom said.

I sighed and set the cupcake down on the counter. "Well, I can't really help that, because—soaked," I explained.

"I'll get you a towel," Tali said, and turned to leave the kitchen in a whirl of pink ruffles.

"Did you remember to go to Mr. Levy's shop?" Mom asked.

"Of course. I went there first."

"I need you to pick up the place cards at the stationery shop as well," Mom said. "But that can wait until tomorrow," she added hastily, apparently reminding herself—again—that it was my birthday.

"Another errand?" I groaned.

"Tali's *quinceañera* is a big day for our family," Mom chided me. "We all need to pitch in. It will be your turn soon enough, *mija*," she added.

"Ugh, don't remind me," I said as Tali reappeared. No part of me was looking forward to wearing a dress like that, even if it did fit.

"Here," Tali said, handing me a small towel. "I'm sorry you got drenched picking up my party stuff, Ana," she added in her thoughtful Tali way.

"It's okay," I answered, using the towel to stop my hair from dripping onto the floor. "The drenching part actually happened while I was walking Osito."

Mom *tsk*'ed again. I figured now was probably not the best time to ask to go to the dog shelter today.

"So what's with your dress?" I asked Talisa, changing the subject. "I thought Mrs. Vega took your measurements?"

Tali shook her head. "Mrs. Vega accidentally swapped the

measurements with Alison Ochoa's," she said. Her eyes filled with tears, which wasn't too surprising. Tali was very sensitive, and it didn't take much to make her cry. Especially, it seemed, when it came to her *quinceañera*. Right away, I felt bad for being huffy before. "Mami called her and . . ." Tali trailed off.

"I called her and gave her a piece of my mind is what I did," Mom proclaimed, hands on hips.

Tali sniffled and I put my hand on her shoulder. "I'm sure Mrs. Vega will fix the dress," I assured her. "Besides, you look pretty no matter what."

That was true; Tali was beautiful, with long dark hair and flawless skin. I glanced over at Mom, who was examining the bag from Mr. Levy's. Mom and Tali could have almost passed for sisters; our Mami looked exactly the same as she did in old photos I'd seen of her from when she'd first moved to New York City from Puerto Rico and married Papi. My dad, on the other hand, already had gray hair (possibly, I'd sometimes think with a smirk, as a result of living with our mother for so many years).

"Oh no!" Mom wailed.

"What?" I asked, a sense of foreboding prickling its way up my spine.

"What is *this*?" She held up what looked like a giant pink candle that had melted in the sun. Bits of tissue paper were coming unstuck from the goopy mess and traveling down her arm.

"It's the piñata for Tali's quince," I said in a small voice. *Here it comes*, I thought.

"But what did you do to it?"

"I didn't *do* anything!" I said, feeling the heat rise on my neck. "I got caught in a giant storm, remember? I'm lucky I didn't get struck by lightning!"

Mom plopped the soggy mess back into the big plastic bag with a huff. "I just don't understand how these things always happen to you."

"It was *rain*. It definitely didn't happen just to me. Anybody who was out there got soaked. And I guess piñatas aren't waterproof," I added.

"Well, they're paper mache," Tali piped up. "Which is mostly made of flour, so it makes sense that it would . . . melt." She added the last part in a weaker voice, as Mom continued to glare at me. "It's not Ana's fault!" my sister added loyally. My sister turned to me. "I'm sorry I ever asked for a piñata, Ana. I only thought it would be fun to have one at the party for our little cousins."

I smiled at my thoughtful sister so she'd know I understood.

Mom was shaking her head. "I'm not blaming you for the rain, Ana. But if you didn't spend so much time with that dog . . ."

My heart sank. My plan to ask to go to the shelter for my birthday wish seemed pretty stupid now. Mom would *never* say yes. She was barely even letting me take care of Osito, and he lived upstairs, not here in our apartment.

Mom must have seen how upset I looked, because she added quickly, "Why don't you go change out of your wet clothes and then you can have your cupcake?"

"I'll go change, too," Tali said. "I can't wait to get out of this ginormous dress."

My sister and I left the kitchen and headed into our shared bedroom. Tali took my arm.

"Cheer up, *hermanita*," Tali said.

I smiled gratefully at her. "Thanks, T. Do you need help getting out of your dress?"

She grinned and closed our bedroom door. "If it fit, I'd need help with the zipper. But now, nope!" To demonstrate, she shimmied side to side and the whole thing fell right down off her body.

I laughed, and began peeling off my wet sweater. "So, Tali . . . I just sort of . . . met someone in the park."

"Ooh—a boy?" Tali sounded much too excited, and I immediately regretted my impulsive confession. My sister was forever falling in crush with a new boy, and she often pestered me, asking which boys at school I liked, and sometimes I'd tell her about a boy I thought was cute, mostly just to have something to say. I'd never actually had anyone to tell her about. Until today.

Tali put on a T-shirt and jeans and bounded across the room to plop on my bed. "Tell me everything!" she said, bouncing up and down.

"Calm down—there's not that much to tell!" I said. "I met him in the dog park. His name is Calvin . . ."

"That's a great name!"

"It's pretty good, I guess," I said, struggling to take my jeans off. There was nothing worse than soaking-wet denim. "He has a pug named Pancake."

"Now *that's* a great name!" Tali exclaimed, and I had to laugh. My sister was always in such a hurry to approve of everyone and everything. I wished for the millionth time that I was more like her. But no amount of wishing would make me different. As Papi always said, like it or no, I took after Mami. I usually saw the flaws first.

A small voice in my head reminded me that I hadn't seen any flaws in Calvin, though.

"Ana Ramos! You have an *actual* dreamy look on your face. You like this boy!" Tali was back to bouncing on the edge of the bed. "Meeting in the rain . . . it's like a fairy tale."

I threw one wet sock at her and she laughed and ducked. "I don't even *know* him. And we only met because his dog liked Osito. Besides, I'm hardly a princess in a fairy tale."

Tali ignored my last comment. "I'm so excited for you, Ana! You're always too busy coming up with new website ideas or cracking codes to pay attention to boys."

I blew a lock of wet hair out of my face. "So, for the billionth time, it's *writing* code." Tali shared a room with me—she knew better than anyone how much I wanted to be a software engineer, and how many hours I spent on my computer trying to master coding.

Tali laughed. "I know, I know. I just like to tease you. Tell me the rest of the story."

"Okay, so . . . he carried that giant piñata bag for me. I didn't even have to ask."

"A gentleman. That's so rare these days," Tali said, lying back on my bed with a sigh.

I rolled my eyes, even though I'd *sort* of had the same thought about Calvin myself. "You sound like you just walked out of a Disney cartoon," I teased Tali. "But that's nothing new. I won't be surprised if one day I look over and there's a ring of cartoon birdies flying in a circle around your head. Actually, maybe you should sing a song to try to summon some. They could fix your dress for you like in *Cinderella*."

It was Tali's turn to throw the wet sock back at me. "Ana, you're ridiculous."

I put on my robe. "Don't blow this Calvin thing out of proportion," I told my sister. "He was just . . . different, that's all. Not like other boys." Tali was regarding me with her best older-sister smile, and I shook my head. "Besides, I might not even see him again. I know Mom's one step away from making me tell Mrs. Ramirez that I can't walk Osito anymore . . ." I didn't even bring up the hopes about getting my own dog. They seemed completely out of reach now.

"No!" Tali said. "Mom wouldn't do that. Mrs. Ramirez—and Osito—need you."

"Paper mache is not waterproof, though," I said with a frown. "Just one mark against me on Mom's very long list."

"List shmist," Tali said. "True love is all about overcoming barriers. Now go take a shower before you catch a cold. You don't want to see Calvin again with a bright red nose with snot coming out of it."

"Thanks for that image," I said with a laugh, and left our room. Even as I rolled my eyes at Tali, there was a tiny part of me that got excited flutters when I did think about meeting Calvin again someday.

4

Someday = Monday

My best friend since kindergarten, Phoebe Yamada, met me at my locker Monday morning.

"Happy belated birthday!" she cried, giving me a huge hug.

Normally, Phoebe and I would have hung out on my birthday, but she and her family had been away this weekend, visiting relatives way upstate. She hadn't been able to get Wi-Fi up there in the woods, so we hadn't even gotten a chance to text.

"This is for you," Phoebe added, handing me a small wrapped box.

"Aw, thanks, Phoebe," I said, carefully opening it. Inside, on a small square of cotton, was a pair of adorable stud earrings in the shape of pugs. I squealed and threw my arms around Phoebe. "They're perfect!" I exclaimed. I quickly removed the silver studs I'd put in earlier that morning and swapped in the new earrings, grinning the whole time.

Phoebe laughed. "I figured it was a way to celebrate your actually getting your own dog . . ." She trailed off and peered at me. "Wait. You *did* ask your parents, right? You went to the dog shelter and everything?"

I looked down at my shoes. "Well . . ."

"You didn't even ask, did you? Ana, I thought you were going to go for it this time!"

"I was . . . but then there was a storm, and the piñata for Tali's party got ruined, and I just . . ."

"You chickened out."

"I . . . yes." Phoebe's disappointed face made it all so much worse. I knew *she* would never have chickened out. This was what always happened. Phoebe was the bold one in our friendship. So she'd build me up and make me think I could be brave enough . . . but then when it was just me, a lot of the time, I wasn't.

Phoebe sighed. "You'll find the right time to ask, I know it."

I gave my best friend a grateful smile. "So where *did* you go for your birthday?" she asked.

"Just to Hi Thai for dinner."

"Aw, A, I'm sorry. I know how much you wanted a dog."

I nodded, feeling a small pang. In the end, my birthday hadn't been all that bad. It was always fun going out to dinner with my family, and we hadn't even talked about Tali's quince *that* much over our pad thai and chicken curries. Plus, I had gotten really nice gifts: a new phone case from my parents, and sunglasses from Tali. I was grateful . . . but I couldn't stop dreaming of a puppy all my own.

The bell rang then, and it was time for our first class, US History with Mr. Bowen.

"So did you hear the latest?" Phoebe asked as we walked down the hall. Phoebe was somehow always up to date on school gossip, even when she'd been away for the weekend. "Mrs. Bahar is finally having her baby, so we're going to have a sub for English for the rest of the year, but I don't know who it'll be."

"I hope the sub is nice," I said. Mrs. Bahar could be strict.

Phoebe nodded. "Oh, and there's a new kid in our grade! He starts today."

"Really?" I said as we turned the corner, moving past the crowds of kids streaming through our middle school. *A new kid? Hmm . . .*

"He's from Florida, somebody said—man, is he going to freeze if he's never lived anywhere cold," Phoebe remarked. "I visited my grandma in Vero Beach last winter break—remember? And it was sooo warm, I almost couldn't believe it, I mean, it was February and I'm pretty sure it got to at least eighty-five . . ."

"Phoebe!" I broke in, curious to hear about the new boy, not Phoebe's grandmother in Vero Beach. "What else did you hear about the new kid?"

"Oh, just that he has blond hair and Lucy Alvarez said he was cute. Of course, she thinks every other boy in America is cute. That girl has very lax standards, if you ask me."

I smiled. Phoebe had never been a fan of Lucy Alvarez, who was one of the prettiest girls in our grade, and one of the most popular.

"Blond hair, huh?" I said. I let out a sigh, though I wasn't sure if I felt relief or disappointment.

Calvin's hair had been brown.

Phoebe and I walked into history class. Math and science were my favorite subjects, but Mr. Bowen was such a good teacher that I'd started loving history this year. I liked how Mr. Bowen seemed to know absolutely everything about American history, and he had high standards. Some of our other teachers, in my humble opinion, let us middle schoolers off way too easy. But not Mr. Bowen.

Phoebe and I took our seats, which were at the front of the class. Even though Phoebe liked the back better, I'd stood firm on this one. I was reaching into my backpack for my notebook and pen when I heard Mr. Bowen say, "We have a new student today, class."

I looked up, expecting to see the unknown blond boy that apparently Lucy Alvarez had found cute.

But then I saw the boy *I* had found cute at the dog park on Saturday. It was Calvin.

"Hair looks darker when it's wet," I said aloud, luckily under my breath.

"What?" Phoebe gave me a look like she thought I was going crazy.

But I wasn't paying any attention to her. I was staring at Calvin. He didn't seem to have noticed me yet.

"Please join me in welcoming Calvin Palmer to our class," Mr. Bowen went on. "He's moved here all the way from Florida."

"Hi, Calvin," everyone said in chorus.

Mr. Bowen pointed to the open seat on the other side of the room, and Calvin headed for it. I tensed up. He still hadn't seen me. *Would he even recognize me?* I wondered. My dark brown hair couldn't have looked much darker even when soaking wet, but maybe I looked different now that I was all dried off.

"We've just finished World War II," Mr. Bowen told Calvin. "So we're about to start our study of . . ."

"The Cold War and Korea?" Calvin jumped in to ask.

"Very good!" Mr. Bowen said. "Today, we'll be discussing the Korean War. First, let's see if everyone remembers their reading from last night."

I had the notes I'd taken last night open and ready to go. I skimmed them briefly while still keeping an ear out for Mr. Bowen's first question. Phoebe often called me the Hermione Granger of MS 110. But I ignored her teasing—not only did I like being first in our class, it was important for me to keep that standing. I'd been working hard to earn the Crown Point Prize, which went to the top student in each grade, and paid for a prestigious computer summer camp program. Aside from getting a dog, attending that program was my biggest dream.

"From 1910 until the closing days of World War II," Mr. Bowen was saying, "Korea was ruled by . . . ?"

I raised my hand high. But so did Calvin. With a look of surprise, Mr. Bowen called on him.

"They were ruled by Japan," Calvin responded confidently. "Then after World War II, the Soviet Union wanted to establish a communist government in Korea. But the United States wanted to stop the spread of communism. So Korea ended up being split into two separate countries, North and South Korea."

"That's very good!" Mr. Bowen said enthusiastically.

"Who *is* this kid?" Phoebe whispered to me, rolling her eyes.

"You must have been studying this topic at your school in Florida?" Mr. Bowen asked Calvin.

"No, we were still on World War II. I just really like reading about history."

Seriously? Who *was* this kid? Then I had another thought, and it was like Phoebe read my mind. My best friend turned to me and whisper-hissed, "I think you have some competition!"

I nodded, trying to ignore the sense of dread I felt stirring in me.

"That's excellent, Calvin," Mr. Bowen was saying. "Class, can anyone tell me where Korea was divided?"

"The thirty-eighth parallel!" I burst out, forgetting to wait for Mr. Bowen to even call on me.

At that moment, Calvin noticed me. And he must have recognized me, because he grinned at me.

I smiled back, but a big part of me was thinking that Phoebe was right. Not only was Calvin cute, and nice . . . he was also really smart—and he was definitely going to be competition for my slot at the top of our class.

*　　*　　*

"New kid was like Answer Boy today, huh?" Phoebe asked at lunch, biting into her cheese sandwich. "I mean, take a break and let someone else say something."

"That's usually me who's always answering in class," I said, unwrapping my turkey sandwich. "You realize that, right?"

Phoebe waved a dismissive hand in the air. "You're overly prepared, sure. But this guy like full-on admitted that he hadn't even studied this stuff at his school yet. I mean, come on, what kind of nerd . . ."

"Hi, Calvin," I said, much too brightly and loudly. Because there he stood beside our lunch table, looking just as cute as he had on Saturday. Maybe even cuter all dried off.

"Hi, Ana," he said. "I can't believe we go to the same school—we're even in the same grade! Small world, huh?"

"The smallest," I agreed, feeling my heart skip a beat.

"Hi, I'm Phoebe Yamada," Phoebe said, reaching across the table to shake Calvin's hand. "So you two already know each other?" she added, with a very pointed look at me.

Oops—that was right. I hadn't gotten a chance to tell Phoebe about my run-in with Calvin over the weekend.

"Ana and I met at the dog park the other day," Calvin explained.

"Oh, when you were walking Osito?" Phoebe asked me, and I nodded, suddenly worried Phoebe might say something about Mrs. Ramirez before I had a chance to explain. Thankfully, she turned her attention back to Calvin. "So you moved here from Florida?" she asked him.

"Can I sit?" Calvin asked, holding up his lunch bag.

"Sorry," I said, shooting Phoebe a look now. "Of course you can sit."

Calvin sat down beside me, which made me a little nervous, but I tried not to show it. I took a sip of my chocolate milk.

"Yeah, we just moved from Tampa," Calvin said, unwrapping his sandwich.

"You must think it's so cold here," Phoebe told him.

"Well, it's April, so it's not so bad," Calvin said, and shot me a small smile. "But maybe ask me in January."

"Do you have a big family?" Phoebe asked. I thought it was kind of ironic that Phoebe had called Calvin Answer Boy a few minutes ago, since now she was acting like Question Girl.

"I have an older sister, but she's away at college. How about you guys?"

"I'm an only, but Ana has an older sister, too."

"Another thing we have in common," Calvin said to me.

"Another thing?" Phoebe asked.

"We both love pugs," Calvin said.

"Your dog's a pug, huh?"

Calvin nodded. "Best dogs in the world."

"So how do you like New York?" I jumped in to ask him, hoping to steer the conversation away from pugs. I was also curious as to what he would say. I, for one, couldn't imagine being from anywhere else. I'd lived in the city my whole life—we'd even lived in our same apartment on Avenue C since I was two.

A shadow seemed to pass over Calvin's face, but then he replaced it with a smile. "It's really different from where we used to live," he admitted. "I haven't seen much so far, with the move and school and everything. I'm actually saving up for a bike. Then I'll be able to see more of the city."

The lunch dismissal bell rang. Phoebe got to her feet and I turned to Calvin, gathering up my courage.

"I'm glad you go to our school," I told Calvin in a rush. "Now I know for sure I'll see you again."

He nodded. "And probably at the dog park later, too."

"Probably," I agreed. But I didn't get to say any more since Phoebe had already started walking toward the doors. I stood up from the table. "Well, bye."

"Bye," Calvin said.

"Where's the fire?" I asked Phoebe when we reached the hallway.

"No fire. I just don't want to be late for coding and get stuck with the slow computer again."

"Calvin seems really nice, doesn't he?"

Phoebe gave me a strange look. "Yeah. But did you forget his performance in Bowen's class? Maybe you shouldn't get too attached. I mean, I'd hate to see you lose out on the prize to some kid who just showed up halfway through the year."

I nodded, frowning as her words sank in. I knew Phoebe was right. My biggest competition up until now had been Laila Abadi, who was practically a genius. I had a slightly higher grade point average than she did. But now here was Calvin.

"Computer summer program. Bronx High School of Science. Scholarship to MIT. Software engineering gig at Google or somewhere equally amazing." Phoebe repeated my own mantra to me. "My advice? Don't let some random boy from Florida get in the way of that. No matter how cute." She added the last part with a raised eyebrow, as though daring me to contradict—or admit—her claim that Calvin was cute.

"He is cute," I told her, holding her gaze. "But you're right. Nothing gets in the way."

"That's my girl," Phoebe said, linking arms as we walked down the hall.

"And *you're* gonna get a scholarship to USC and be a show runner on your own TV show by the age of twenty-five." I recited Phoebe's mantra back to her and she nodded with a determined look on her face.

"I've been thinking I should change the age to thirty," she said. "I know that sounds super old, but what if I'm already writing for a successful show? Might learn some more tricks of the trade before I start my own."

"Good call." I nudged her. "I can't wait to visit you on set. I'll know someone famous."

"The writers aren't famous," Phoebe said. "But I'll know the actors, and they *will* be famous!"

I grinned. It was always fun to talk about the future with Phoebe.

As we walked into coding class and I took a seat at my computer station, I thought about Calvin again. I wondered if he'd be in any more of my classes, so I could see just how good of a student he was. Maybe he was only great at history. Then my mind flashed back to how sweet he'd been on Saturday, when he'd carried my bag for me in the rain.

As if I'd caused him to appear with the power of my thoughts, Calvin walked in the door to coding class.

"Hi again," he said. "Mind if I sit with you guys?"

Phoebe raised her eyebrows but didn't say anything else.

"I don't mind," I told him. And the problem was, even with the potential competition brewing, I really didn't.

Ms. Vasquez came rushing in just as the bell was ringing.

"Okay, class," she said, "everybody please navigate to our training page for Ruby."

I loved coding class, but I already knew Ruby really well—I was hoping to learn a new language, like Scratch. Ms. V had promised she'd set something up for me, but when I glanced beside me and saw Calvin's look of confusion, I knew what I'd be doing that class period. I often ended up helping out my classmates.

"I'll show you how to get to the site," I told him. I gestured to Calvin's keyboard and he nodded gratefully and moved a little out of the way so I could type.

I was showing Calvin how to navigate the training site when Ms. Vasquez came to stand behind us.

"You must be Calvin," she said. "Welcome to the class. You're on the right track already—just stick with Ana and you'll be coding like a pro in no time. She's my star student." Ms. V gave me a wink and I smiled, feeling a warm glow.

"Thanks, Ana," Calvin said to me, and my glow turned into a blush.

"You've never done this before, huh?" Phoebe leaned over me to ask Calvin.

"No, we didn't have a coding class at my old school. But it sounds really interesting."

"Well, I don't know how you'll ever catch up on everything you missed all year," Phoebe said. "But Ms. V's right—if anybody can help you, it's Ana," she added with a grin, then returned to her own computer.

"Don't listen to Phoebe," I told Calvin. "You'll catch up."

I started typing fast, entering all the registration stuff for Calvin—his name and the school's address.

"Sometimes I don't think I'll ever move fast enough to catch up in this place," Calvin said softly, too low for anybody but me to hear. When I looked up, I expected him to look sad or upset, but he was wearing his usual smile again. "Okay," he said. "Let's go—I'm ready to code!"

But his quiet comment stayed with me, and it seemed to me that *that* had been the truth, and not the confident smile he'd put back on his face a few seconds later.

WEBSITE DESIGN IDEAS

IDEA #1:

Site for taking homework notes.

Function: Type notes into a template on the site that is then searchable by key words, to answer questions quickly in class.

Working-title ideas:

Notesearch

Searchable Homework

~~Just Call Me Hermione~~

5

Fake Fish Emergency

After school that day, in the park, I ran right into Calvin.

He was coming out of the double gates to the dog run. I was looking down, trying to get the outer gate open—not realizing that it wasn't opening because Calvin was pushing the other way.

I looked up in surprise and we both laughed.

"Ana!" Calvin said. "Hey, we almost missed you. Pancake and I were about to head home. But we can hang out for a few more minutes."

"That'd be great," I said, recovering from my surprise and following him back into the dog run. Osito hurried forward, straining at his leash and barking at Pancake. I laughed as Pancake barked right back. I unclipped Osito's leash, and Calvin did the same for Pancake. We watched as the two pugs dashed off together, jumping and playing. It was too cute.

"What are you drinking?" I asked Calvin. He was holding a half-full tumbler with a lid, and the liquid inside was bright green.

"A smoothie. My mom came up with the recipe for this one—she calls it The Hulk."

"Huh. Well, it looks very . . . healthy. So how was your first day at MS 110?" I asked.

"Good. I really liked a couple of the teachers so far. Mr. Bowen seems really nice."

"Yeah. He's great."

"Is history your favorite subject?" Calvin asked.

"Nah, that's got to be coding class. I want to be a software engineer someday."

"I should have guessed that, based on how good you are at coding," Calvin said, and I blushed again. I wished I wouldn't do that so much.

I glanced over at Osito and Pancake. Now they were rolling around and around together like a big round pug ball. I giggled.

Calvin started laughing, too. "Must be nice to be a dog. You just have to play, eat, and sleep. Though I guess it would get boring."

"Probably. Dogs can't read about history."

"Or write code."

"Do you think you want to study history when you get older?" I asked Calvin.

"Maybe," he said. "My ultimate dream would be to work at the United Nations—ultimate-ultimate would be to sit on the UN Security Council."

I was impressed. Calvin was obviously smart, and like me, he had big plans. That wasn't too common with kids our age, I knew. But then I heard Phoebe's voice in my head saying: *Competition!*

Calvin's phone buzzed and he glanced down at the screen. "Oh, that's my dad," he said. "Pancake and I should head home now."

I was surprised to feel a swell of disappointment.

"But, hey," Calvin added, brightening. "You and Osito could come with us—for dinner? Pancake and Osito could have, what do they call it with little kids? A playdate! Pancake really seems to love playing with Osito . . ." He didn't have to finish his sentence, just gestured to the two of them, still playing happily. Now they were running circles around a stick together.

Dinner? My mind raced. My parents might allow me to go to dinner at a classmate's house last minute. But what would I tell Mrs. Ramirez about Osito? She was expecting him home in a few minutes.

"Um, I'd love to," I said, frantically trying to come up with an excuse, "but I'll have to take a rain check. I promised my sister I'd help her clean out her . . . aquarium tonight."

What? I cringed at my own words. Tali didn't have an *aquarium*, for crying out loud.

"Oh," Calvin said. "Okay, well, if it's a fish emergency."

"It's not an *emergency* exactly, but I promised, you know, and it gets pretty dirty in there, and the water is like their air. Can you imagine trying to breathe dirty air . . . ?" I trailed off. Why was I so terrible at lying? And worse than that, why was I even lying in the first place?

But Calvin was putting Pancake back into her harness. "Some other time," he said. Then he was waving good-bye . . . he was walking away, and I'd lost my moment to admit that Osito belonged to my neighbor, so that was why I had to take him back. The thought of running after Calvin and confessing . . . *now* . . . seemed ridiculous.

"See you at school tomorrow," Calvin called over his shoulder. I watched him head west. Then I gathered up a forlorn-looking Osito and headed toward home.

I delivered Osito back to Mrs. R, and then went downstairs and got to work on my history homework. No matter how nice Calvin was, I still had no intention of not knowing the answer to any of Mr. Bowen's questions tomorrow in class.

Mom called me to come out for dinner. I went into the kitchen, where Tali was moving party supplies off the table so she could put down our place settings.

My mouth started watering as Mom carried over a big

platter of *pollo horneado*—baked chicken. Papi followed with a big bowl filled with salad. Talisa went to the fridge, coming back with two bottles of salad dressing.

"*Gracias, mija*," Mom told her. She usually only used Spanish when she was either angry or annoyed—or when she was feeling very happy. Based on the mess that surrounded us, I had a feeling it wasn't the last one.

"So how was everyone's day?" Papi asked as we all sat down and dug into our meal.

Well, I'm still a little upset about my disappointing birthday. I'm still a lot upset at myself for chickening out on asking for a rescue dog. I'm worried the new boy in school will be my competition for the Crown Point Prize. I'm also worried that I find this new boy cute. AND I'm trying to figure out why I told this same new boy that I had to help Tali with her AQUARIUM.

"Fine," I said aloud. Wow, this lying thing was really a slippery slope.

"How about you, Talisa?" Papi asked.

"It was okay. But I have a polynomials quiz tomorrow and I'm pretty sure I'm *not* going to crush it."

Both our parents looked confused for a second, but then they clearly figured out what Tali meant. English was my parents' second language, so they didn't always get our expressions—such as what "crushing" or "not crushing" something was all about.

"Your sister can help you," Mom said. "She's very good in math."

Tali groaned. "But Ana's still in middle school. I'm in tenth grade. If she can do my homework, I'm quitting school right now."

I concentrated on my chicken and didn't say what I'd been about to say, which was that I probably *could* help Tali. We'd done some polynomials in my intro to algebra class this year.

"And how about your day, Teresa?" Papi asked Mami.

Our Mami gave a groan of her own and started telling Papi about her day at work in rapid Spanish. She worked at a doctor's office, and to hear her stories, the other girls who worked there—she always called them *girls*—were just about useless. Then she switched to English and started listing all the things she'd gotten in the past couple of days for Tali's party.

"We've got the napkins, and the string lights finally came in, though one had a bulb out so I have to send them back, which is a pain but at least we have time."

"You bought the string lights after all?" Papi asked. "I thought we talked about trying to borrow some?"

Mom sighed. "Whatever we get now we can use for Ana's quince, too."

"Great," I said. "Now not only do I have this giant fluffy party to look forward to, but everything at the party will be hand-me-downs?"

I got a sharp look from Mom, but then her features softened. "*Hija*. Is this about me forgetting your cupcake? I told you I was sorry, and I meant it."

"I know." I waved a hand in the air. "It's not about that. It's just all this quince craziness. It's taking over the house and it's still like a month away."

"Don't worry—we'll make just as big a fuss for your fifteenth," Papi said.

"That's what I'm afraid of," I said.

6

I Didn't Choose the Pug Life . . . the Pug Life Chose Me

My fishy lie didn't buy me much time. The next morning, when I was at my locker, Calvin appeared and invited Osito and me over for some pug bonding on Saturday.

I'd been ready to set Calvin straight about Osito being my neighbor's dog. Even though I knew I'd waited too long, and it was officially weird now, I'd still decided to come clean. My awkward fib about helping Tali with her nonexistent aquarium kept echoing in my head, and it made me feel embarrassed and kind of uncomfortable.

But then Calvin explained why he was so set on Osito coming to play with Pancake.

"So the thing is, Pancake's been ... depressed, I guess?" Calvin said as we stood facing each other. "Ever since we moved here. She used to be so playful, but lately she just lies on the floor and looks up at me with these sad eyes. But not when your dog's around."

"I, so—" I cleared my throat, getting ready to say that Osito, wasn't, um, *my* dog. But Calvin continued, clearly intent on sharing his worries about Pancake.

"When she's with Osito, it's like Pancake's back to her old self. So I was hoping they could spend some more time together. Maybe help pull Pancake out of her funk."

How could I say no to that? First of all, Osito himself had seemed down lately, and he definitely perked up around Pancake. Plus, it broke my heart to think of Pancake being sad.

I also remembered the look that had passed over Calvin's face when I'd asked him how he was liking New York City. And his quiet comment in coding class. I had to wonder if maybe Calvin wasn't having all that easy of a transition, either.

"I'll ask my parents to make sure, but, yeah—that sounds great," I said. "Osito would love it."

"Great," Calvin said, his face breaking into an adorable smile that made my heart flip over. "Let's exchange numbers now so we can text each other on Saturday if we need to."

I'd never traded phone numbers with a boy before, but I tried to act calm as I gave Calvin my number and then he gave me his. *It's all for the pugs*, I told myself.

When we were done, Calvin gave me a me a thumbs-up and then headed away toward his own locker.

I bit my lip, thinking ahead to Saturday. I usually took Osito for his walks early in the morning and in the afternoon. Never during dinnertime. I had to figure out what I was going to say to Mrs. Ramirez so that "my" dog could go cheer up Calvin's dog. Maybe with a little planning I could come up with something convincing.

I was on my way to lunch when Calvin texted me.

It was a meme: a sad-faced pug being forced to wear a ridiculous frog costume.

I stifled a giggle and started searching for something to send back. I saw that there were a *lot* of pug memes out there, so I chose one: another grumpy-faced pug, this time with the phrase I DIDN'T CHOOSE THE PUG LIFE—THE PUG LIFE CHOSE ME.

I was sitting down in the cafeteria when a new text from Calvin came in. This one was a screenshot of an Instagram post. The account was called potato_the_pug and the profile picture was of a cute light brown pug that looked a little like Pancake. The dog was wearing a bumblebee costume, and his sad, wrinkly face made me laugh out loud.

"What are you doing?" Phoebe asked as she sat down across from me.

"Nothing," I said, putting my phone away. For some reason I didn't feel like sharing what Calvin had sent me, even with Phoebe.

I stayed up way past my bedtime finishing my English paper (it turned out the substitute we got was even tougher than Mrs. Bahar). Luckily my sister was able to fall asleep when I still had the light on.

I woke up the next morning feeling tired and bleary-eyed, wishing for another hour or so of sleep. Mom came into my room and told me that Mrs. Ramirez had already called to ask if I would walk Osito before school. Her back was hurting especially bad and she wasn't sure if she could manage the stairs, Mom said. I felt a pang of sympathy. Since our building was a walk-up, there was no elevator, and Mrs. R's apartment was on the fifth floor. She and her late husband had moved in many years ago, I knew, and the apartment was rent-controlled, so moving to a different apartment was probably out of the question.

For selfish reasons, though, I hoped that Mrs. R *wouldn't* move. As I pulled on my jeans and sweater I thought about what would happen if she did. Mrs. R had told me many times that if she had to give up her apartment, she would go live with her daughter in Baltimore. And then I'd probably never see my little bear again. The thought hurt my heart, but I pushed it back and quickly tied my sneakers. There was no use worrying about the possibility of Osito moving away—there was nothing I could do about it.

I crept out of our still-quiet apartment and climbed the flight of stairs to Mrs. R's.

When I unlocked her door, Osito was waiting. He wagged his tail at the sight of me and I scratched behind his ears.

"I'm here to take O!" I called. "We'll be right back."

I heard a weak "Thank you, Ana" coming from the direction of the bedroom.

I started trying to get the wriggly little ball of black fur into his harness, but then he pulled one of his tricks: rolling over onto his back. Osito wriggled around, his black eyes sparkling, and very clearly sending one message loud and clear: PET ME. I knelt beside him and scratched his belly as he continued to wriggle in delight. Then I stood up to show him it was time to go.

"Come on, Osito," I told him. "I'm sure you have to go to the bathroom, don't you?" But he clearly wasn't finished having his belly scratched. I couldn't help but laugh as I bent down and gave him a couple more scratches, then stood again. Then, the little stinker faked me out by standing up—but when I started to put on his harness he rolled over *again*.

"You're terrible," I told him, then crossed my arms and waited. When he still didn't roll back over, I cracked open the door as though I were going to leave, and he finally stood upright.

I picked him up to carry him quickly down the stairs and outside our building.

As soon as we reached the closest tiny patch of grass, Osito got right down to business. He looked up at me when he was finished, and his huge, round, black eyes still seemed to be trying to communicate with me. I scooped him back up and sat down on a nearby bench with him.

"Oh, Osito, you're such a good, sweet little bear," I told him, planting a kiss on the top of his soft, furry head. He responded by licking my face thoroughly, and I giggled.

I hadn't meant to get quite so attached to Osito. At first it had seemed like a way to get having a dog of my own out of my system, since Mom had never really wavered in her no-pets rule. She liked to keep the apartment spotless, and having something that shed fur and possibly—gasp!—drooled was not an idea she supported.

I stroked the soft fur between his ears a little more. "Okay, let's walk, and then I have to take you back to your Mami," I told him, and set him down on the sidewalk. He trotted happily beside me.

I mentally added a step to my mantra. Computer summer program, Bronx Science, MIT, *dog*, Google. Someday I'd be out on my own, and then I could finally have a dog of my own. Although I couldn't actually imagine loving one more than I loved Osito.

"Hey, A!" Phoebe greeted me when I got to her locker. "You're late today."

"Sorry. I had to walk Osito this morning for Mrs. R."

Phoebe rolled her eyes. "He should just be your dog. I mean . . . poor Mrs. R."

I gave her a half smile. "I sort of agree on both counts, although I feel bad about agreeing with the first part." I shook my head as Phoebe got her books out of her locker. "So . . . speaking of bad, how would you feel about helping me come up with a lie?"

Phoebe cocked her head to one side as we walked down the hall together. "A lie? What for?"

"So I can dognap Osito this Saturday night."

Phoebe gave me a look. "Ana, if you want something to do

on Saturday night, we can go to the movies or something. You don't have to resort to stealing your neighbor's dog."

I snorted. "I *have* plans, thank you very much. I'm invited to Calvin's house for dinner."

Phoebe stopped walking and said *"What?"* so loudly that we got a pointed look from the vice principal, Mr. Rios, as he walked by.

Phoebe put a hand on my arm. "Rewind. You're going on a *date*? With *Calvin*?"

"It's not a date!" I realized I must have yelled that when we got a bunch of curious looks from the other kids in the hall. "It's not like that," I said in a lower voice. "I mean, it's a *play*date. For his dog, Pancake, and Osito."

"I don't get it. Why would Calvin want to have his dog play with your neighbor's dog? That's just . . . weird."

"I agree. It would be weird. Except . . . Calvin thinks Osito is *my* dog."

"Why would he think that?"

We'd reached my locker, and I opened the door and looked inside rather than at Phoebe while I confessed. "At first, when we met in the park, he just assumed. I was going to correct him, but then I accidentally waited too long, and it got to the point where it would have been weird. I was *still* going to tell him, but then Calvin came up to me with this whole plan because his dog has seemed depressed since moving to New York. She's only happy when Osito's around . . . and then I was like, well, dang, I was going to come clean, but isn't it more important to help this dog—and Calvin? I mean, if Osito can make them both happier, and it would be good for Osito, too, since he's almost always stuck up in that apartment with Mrs. R—I mean, that's a win-win-win, right?" I finally looked up.

"The dog's depressed, huh?"

I nodded. "That's what Calvin said."

"New York can be a rough town," Phoebe observed in a grave voice, but she rolled her eyes. I knew Phoebe didn't one hundred percent get my dog obsession. In fact, I suspected that she might grow up to agree with my mother about dog hair on her furniture. "But, A," Phoebe went on, "are you sure there's not more to all of this than just pug charity? Like maybe *you* want to go to Calvin's house?"

I shook my head. "No, it's not about that. I mean he's nice, and . . ."

"Cute."

"I did not say that!"

"Well, you were thinking it."

I tried to will away my blush. "So how about it?" I asked Phoebe as I stuffed my textbooks into my backpack. "Are you too appalled by the lies I've already told to help me figure out a way to get Osito for a few hours on Saturday?"

Phoebe smiled and shook her head. "Nah. I'll help you brainstorm. I mean, at this point it wouldn't help anybody to know O's not really your dog, right? And it's not like you started out *planning* to lie."

I gave Phoebe a grateful smile, then slammed my locker door shut. "Darn right. I didn't choose the pug life. The pug life chose me."

7

The Principle of Least Astonishment

"What if you said you were taking Osito to an audition to be in a commercial?" Phoebe unwrapped her sandwich and took a bite. "For dog food."

"Okay, that's not a bad idea," I said. "I'm sure there are lots of commercials filmed here."

"Actually, I read online there are a lot more filmed in places like Atlanta or Orlando. Cheaper. But it's still plausible."

"What kind of dog food?" I asked, sticking a fork into the cafeteria's gloppy mac and cheese. Mom had forgotten to pack our lunches today because she'd been so busy nailing down some details about Talia's quince.

Phoebe opened her bag of chips, ate one, and then offered some to me. "I think not getting too specific is the key. More of a chance to get tripped up."

"What if Mrs. R doesn't want him to be in a commercial? She might not," I argued.

"True, not everybody's about the showbiz life. And if she says no, then you definitely won't have a way to get him that night." Phoebe drummed her fingers on the table. "What we need is a plan with a relatively low chance of failure. What would Mrs. R definitely say yes to?"

"Well, she wants Osito to get out more. Have more chances for exercise and play . . ."

Phoebe put down the bag of chips. "Um, not to be Captain Obvious here, but how about you just tell her the truth? That a kid in your class has a pug who met Osito at the park and they hit it off—and now you want to take him to a doggy playdate?"

"That's just crazy enough to work!" I said with a laugh. "Was I making things too complicated again?"

"I think maybe. But it depends on if you think Mrs. Ramirez would be, like, weird about Osito going to somebody else's house? Somebody she doesn't know?"

"I don't know. I guess she might be. But," I continued, my mind racing, ". . . she's met *you*. And you only live two blocks away. What if it were *you* who just got a pug . . . ?"

"Now you're overcomplicating again."

"No, I mean, yes, I probably am, but Mrs. R has met you—and your mom that one time, remember? She'd be totally okay with me taking Osito over to your place."

Phoebe was shaking her head. "Oh, what a tangled web."

"Hey, guys, what's up?" Calvin had appeared beside Phoebe.

"Just doing some brainstorming with Charlotte here," Phoebe said, giving me a look.

"Charlotte?" Calvin looked confused.

I knew what Phoebe meant, of course—*Charlotte's Web* . . . of lies.

"It's an old nickname," Phoebe said.

"For *Ana*?"

"Phoebe's really weird," I told him, and she stuck her tongue out at me before standing up.

"So. I'm gonna go," Phoebe said, waving. "We'll talk later about my *adoption*."

"Was Phoebe adopted?" Calvin asked when she had gone.

"Nope, but—remember? Weird."

Calvin still looked confused, but he seemed inclined to let it go. "Did you ask your parents about Saturday?"

"I'll ask them tonight. I was going to, but my mom has been really stressed. Gotta pick your moment, you know."

"I get that," Calvin said with a grin.

I felt a pang of guilt about lying again. But then I decided that a few little white lies were totally worth it to make two dogs—and a boy—happy.

I threw my books down in a jumbled pile on my desk. I wanted to change my clothes quickly and go get Osito for our walk. In coding class, Calvin had said he and Pancake would be at the dog run right after school, and last time he'd beaten me there—probably because he actually lived with his dog.

"Whoa, what's with you?" My sister looked up from her homework.

"Nothing."

Tali shook her head. "Nah, I don't buy it. You're usually much nicer to the books. The books are your friends."

"I'm just hurrying to get Osito."

"What else is new? I'd step lively to avoid Mom on the way out, then. She said something about this enrichment class at the community center that she wants to sign you up for."

I stopped changing and flopped onto the edge of my bed. "*Another* enrichment class? When am I supposed to cram that in? Between school and Osito—and I still don't have an idea for my big coding project . . . ugh. She just doesn't understand."

"Well, then tell her that. Except maybe leave out the part about Osito. You know she thinks you spend too much time taking care of him."

"Yeah, *time when you could be studying, Ana.* Except, if I study any harder my whole brain's going to explode. What does she want? I've had straight As since birth. But now, it might not even matter, since with Calvin here I might not even get the Crown Point Prize."

"What does Calvin have to do with the prize? Is it because he's *distracting* you?"

I threw my discarded shirt at her. "Ugh, I'm never telling you about a boy ever again. It's not like that. It's just . . . Calvin's really smart. Phoebe and I both think that he might beat me for the first-place slot in our class."

"Oh no! I hadn't thought of that when you told me he was smart. But you're up for a little competition, sis. You've got this."

"I hope so. It's just, lately I feel pulled in so many directions. It's hard to focus."

"A good crush will do that to you."

"I don't have a crush!"

"Are you sure?"

My cheeks burned. "Well, not entirely sure. What's wrong with me? I always used to be sure about stuff."

"Nobody's sure about everything all the time, Ana." Tali's phone buzzed with a text and she reached for it.

"Oh my gosh, what time is it?" I asked, shucking off the other leg of my tights and pulling a clean pair of jeans from my drawer.

"4:12. What's the rush?"

"I need to go get Osito, remember?" I started tying my sneakers as fast as I could.

"I'm sure he'll be okay for a couple more minutes. Oh, unless you have a certain *appointment* at the dog park," she added with a wink.

I stuck my tongue out at her. "I repeat: I am never telling you about another boy, ever again!"

"We both know that's not true. Okay, go. Tell Calvin and Fruitcake I said hi!"

I spun around to pause in the doorway. "It's *Pan*cake."

"I know," Tali said. "I just like that face you make when you think someone's made a mistake. Your eyes bug out and your neck goes all splotchy."

"You're secretly evil, aren't you? Everyone thinks you're the sweetest person in America, but it's all an act, isn't it?"

"Mwahaha." Tali tried for an evil laugh. "Tell no one."

"Right. Like anyone would believe me. Later."

I sprinted out of the apartment and raced upstairs to Mrs. Ramirez's. I was relieved to find that she wasn't home to answer my knock—it meant she'd felt well enough to go to work again today. I let myself in to find a very excited little bear.

"Oh my gosh, I missed you, too, Osito!" I said as I knelt down to receive a very thorough face-licking. "Okay, okay, let's get your harness on and get you to the park for some playtime! If we hurry your friend Pancake might still be there."

I closed his harness, hooked up his leash, and scooped him up to carry him down the stairs. I kept carrying him for a little while after we stepped out of the building, to make better time. But he gave a soft whimper, and I knew that, having been cooped up all day, he wanted to be down to walk on his own and be free to sniff. So I put him down and our pace slowed to match his short legs.

When we got to the park, Calvin wasn't there. I let Osito play with the other small dogs for longer than usual, but Calvin and Pancake never showed. I knew we must have missed them. Finally, I had to get home to work on my essay for Mr. Bowen. I had a fleeting thought that Calvin had probably hurried up his time in the park with Pancake for the very same reason.

I knew I should scoop up Osito and double-time it home, but instead I followed along slowly behind the little pug. I felt deflated, or maybe like Tali's piñata that had melted in the storm. The day I'd met Calvin . . .

I stopped walking then, and picked up Osito. I started marching home as fast as I could. *You are done being ridiculous over a boy, Ana Julieta Ramos. No matter how cute he . . . his dog is. Get it together.*

As soon as I got home, I sat down at the computer for the rest of the night and I set out to write the best darn essay that Mr. Bowen had ever seen.

Eyes on the prize, Ramos, I kept telling myself.

I couldn't let this whole Calvin and Pancake thing take away my academic focus. The time for distractions was over.

The next day, in coding class, Ms. Vasquez was late. Calvin, Phoebe, and I took our usual seats and Calvin glanced at me as I started up my computer.

"I've missed so much in this class—I don't see how I can ever catch up enough to work on that big project," Calvin said to me. It was exactly what I'd suspected was bothering him.

"You'll be fine," I said. "That's the best part about coding— you can make a site that's less complicated—or if you have the skills you can add a lot of functionality. Ms. Vasquez knows you just started—she'll evaluate your work based on how long you've been in the class."

Then a traitorous thought flashed through my mind that it was too bad Calvin's coding grade *wouldn't* be lower. My worry about losing the Crown Point Prize was always there in the back of my mind.

But, despite all that, I found myself saying, "I can always help you, if you want."

"Thanks, Ana," Calvin said.

Ms. Vasquez came rushing in the door then, carrying a big box.

"Guys, good news—thanks to the funds we raised last semester, we get our free T-shirts today," she said.

Last semester, a bunch of us from the class had helped Ms. Vasquez at a fund-raising event for a coding organization.

Phoebe and I had stood at the booth, selling simple magnetic coding toys for young kids that we had designed in class.

"Tell me your size and I'll hook you up with a shirt," Ms. Vasquez said. People started yelling out their sizes, and Ms. Vasquez kept digging around in the box, one by one.

A loud sigh escaped me. "What?" Calvin asked.

"It's just she's doing that in such an inefficient way."

On my other side, Phoebe giggled. "Our girl Ana likes things to be *organized*."

I shot Phoebe a look.

"That's cute," Calvin said. "It's actually bothering you."

And then Phoebe shot *me* a look, no doubt over the word *cute*.

I felt my cheeks grow hotter, then tried to tell myself that I was being extremely silly. After all, Calvin hadn't called *me* cute—he'd called my obsessive need for organization cute. Which wasn't at all the same thing.

Finally, Ms. V gave me, Calvin, and Phoebe our shirts. We started pulling them on over what we were wearing. Calvin looked down at his shirt, which, just like all the others, said I'M A GIRL WHO CODES—ASK ME HOW.

"Huh," Calvin said.

"It's for Girls Who Code," I explained. "It's an organization that Ms. Vasquez supports. That's what we did the fund-raiser for last semester."

"Not manly enough for ya?" Phoebe asked.

Calvin shrugged. "My aunt's an engineer. I can get behind this. Besides," he said, doing a slow turn in front of us and pointing to his T-shirt, "I make this look good."

Phoebe and I both started laughing, and a few minutes later Ms. V finally finished her (very inefficient) T-shirt distribution and started class.

"Today we're going to have a mini-lesson on the history of the programming language Ruby and its creator, Yukihiro Matsumoto," Ms. V began. "Ruby was first released in 1995. I know—forever ago! But it's still a very commonly used language, and especially popular with those new to coding. One great feature of Ruby is that it follows the POLA—can anyone tell me what that means?"

I raised my hand and Ms. V called on me.

"It stands for principle of least astonishment," I answered. "It means that systems should behave the way that users expect them to behave."

"Good! That's why we're learning this language here in Coding I. Now, let's talk a little bit about Matsumoto."

"Wow, that was impressive," Calvin said under his breath while a video clip Ms. V had embedded in her presentation was loading.

"Thanks," I said. I was glad when Ms. V turned the lights off for the video because I was afraid I might be blushing again.

On the other side of me, Phoebe whispered, "You really should start using that principle of least astonishment thing yourself. Like coming up with a way to get Osito on Saturday?" she added.

"Touché," I said.

"What does that mean?"

"It means you're right," I whispered back.

WEBSITE DESIGN IDEAS

IDEA #2:

Study timer.

Functions: Disable social media and other time-suck sites.

Send reminders about assignments due.

Maybe send motivational quotes?

Goal: GET BACK TO WORK ALREADY.

Working-title ideas:

Get to Work, Ana

8

Pug in an Ugg

Mrs. Ramirez was so excited to hear about Phoebe and her "new pug" that she bought a little packet of bones tied with a pink ribbon for her.

When Phoebe came over to study on Saturday morning, I showed her the bag of treats. "Look, I know I'm always hungry, but I'm not eating those," Phoebe said, then laughed at her own joke.

"Ha ha," I said, sitting down on my bed. "I guess I'll take them to the shelter?"

"But why not just give them to Osito?"

I narrowed my eyes at her. "Wait for it . . ."

"Oh, duh—they're *from* Mrs. R." Phoebe pretended to smack her forehead. "And he's *her* actual dog. Okay, so why not just give them to Pancake, then?"

"I don't know," I said. The bones would just be another thing to explain to Calvin. I could say they were a present from me, but that seemed . . . weird.

Phoebe shut her history book. "Did you pick out your outfit for dinner tonight? Meeting the parents for the first time. Big milestone."

"It's a doggy playdate!" I exclaimed, my voice coming out much higher than normal. "The parent part is . . . incidental. I'm just going to wear clothes."

"Well, I have to say I support that idea," Phoebe said drily.

I met Calvin and Pancake at the dog run at five o'clock, with the dognapped Osito on his leash. The two pugs licked each other gleefully, and then we all walked over to Calvin's building on Ninth Street. It was a much newer building than the one I lived in, and a doorman appeared to open the door for us. The elevator we stepped into climbed to the seventh floor almost soundlessly.

"It must be so great to have an elevator," I said.

"Your building doesn't have one?" Calvin asked.

"Nope, it's a walk-up," I said as we stepped out of the elevator with our pugs.

"What floor do you live on?"

"Fifth . . . I mean fourth," I said, blushing. I'd been thinking of how far I had to walk up and down with Osito—since Mrs. R lived on the fifth floor.

Calvin gave me a strange look, no doubt wondering why I'd forgotten what floor I lived on, but he didn't say anything. He unlocked the door to his apartment and we headed inside.

"Oh, this must be Ana! I've been dying to meet you." A tall girl with blonde hair the same color as Calvin's sprang out of a chair and enfolded me in a huge hug. I met Calvin's eyes over her shoulder and he shrugged helplessly.

"I didn't know my sister was going to be home," Calvin said, in a way that almost sounded like an apology. "So Ana, now you've met Chelsea," he said. "She's a hugger."

"It's nice to meet you, Chelsea," I said.

"And who's this?" Chelsea knelt down to pet Osito, and he immediately rolled over on his back, wriggling happily as she scratched his stomach. Pancake barked, wanting to join in on the fun, and Chelsea rubbed her tummy as well.

A woman who looked a lot like both Calvin and Chelsea came out of the kitchen. She was wearing a green apron that said ROMAINE CALM—COOK ON with a picture of a head of lettuce with eyes and a mouth underneath it.

"Hi there," the woman said. "You must be Ana. We've heard so much about you."

Calvin had told his mom about me? "Hi, Mrs. Palmer. It's nice to meet you. And thank you for having me."

"You remember that Ana's staying for dinner, right?" Calvin asked her.

"Of course, sweetie," his mom said with a smile. "We're having lasagna, hope that's okay."

"It's vegetarian," Calvin told me. "We don't eat meat."

"Oh, I didn't know that," I said, thinking back to what I'd seen Calvin eat at lunchtime. I hadn't noticed. "But I don't mind—I like everything. Italian food's actually my favorite, so lasagna sounds great."

"Yeah? I like Mexican food the best. The vegetarian thing was Chelsea's fault originally," Calvin added. "She got a pet chick for Easter when she was five, and when she found out that baby chicks turn into the chickens that people eat . . . well, long story short, eventually we all started living the veggie life."

"I'm glad I'm here to meet you, Ana," Chelsea said. She was still sprawled on the floor petting Osito and Pancake. "I'm going back to school tomorrow morning."

"Where do you go to college?" I asked her.

"GW. George Washington University. In DC," she said.

"On a full scholarship," Calvin added.

"Yeah, but Calvin's the brain in the family," Chelsea told me. "He takes after our mom."

"What does your mom do?" I asked.

"She's a consultant for the government. It's all very top secret."

"Do you mean she's a spy?" I asked, my eyes bugging out. It was becoming clear that Calvin's family was so much cooler than mine.

"No. But I think maybe she used to be . . . ," Chelsea said with a wink.

"Time to eat!" Calvin's mom called. Chelsea hopped up and so did Pancake. Osito turned to look at me, as though asking me what he should do.

"Come on, boy," Calvin said, scooping up Osito and carrying him along with us to the dining room. He set Osito on the floor, and then pulled out a chair for me. Osito gave a sigh and lay down under my chair. Calvin sat beside me and Pancake lay down beside Osito.

Then Calvin's dad appeared and said hi, taking a seat at the table. He was bald, with glasses and a friendly smile.

"Ana, this is my dad. Dad, my friend Ana. From school."

"Are you two in the same grade?" Mr. Palmer asked me as he passed me a basket of bread.

"Uh-huh. We're in the same classes for history, coding, and math."

"You must be pretty smart, then," Chelsea said. "Calvin here's a certified genius."

"Stop, Chels," Calvin said. "Ignore her," he told me. "She's always making fun of me and saying my brain's too big."

"No, it's true—we had him tested and everything!" Chelsea said, earning her pointed looks from both her parents.

"Well, anyway, I'm just glad Calvin's got himself a girlfriend," Chelsea added, and I promptly choked on a big bite of Mrs. Palmer's delicious veggie lasagna. Calvin patted me on the back and glared at his sister.

Mrs. Palmer quickly changed the subject, asking me about the coding class at school.

But even though nobody else brought it up after that, I spent the rest of the meal wondering: Why had Calvin's sister thought I was his girlfriend?

Was coming over to his house for dinner a girlfriend thing to do? Had he used Pancake as an excuse? I thought I was probably being silly to even wonder, but what did I know? Sure, I knew about boyfriends from movies, and Tali had had a few boyfriends, but they'd never come over to have dinner with us.

"Ana?" Calvin's voice broke through my thoughts, and I looked up to find the Palmers all staring curiously at me.

"Do you want some more lasagna?" Mrs. Palmer asked me, and I swiftly shook my head and told her no thank you.

"Should we have dessert yet or do you want to wait a little?" Mr. Palmer. "I got some gelato at a place nearby that a coworker told me about."

"Il Laboratorio?" I asked.

"Yes, that's the one."

"It's really good," I said. "They have all kinds of crazy flavors."

"Calvin tells us you're a native New Yorker. Maybe you've got some other recommendations?" Mrs. Palmer asked.

"Sure. I'll think of some places to tell Calvin."

"I vote gelato a little later." Chelsea patted her stomach. "The food's not nearly this good in the dining hall, so I'm more stuffed than usual."

"Okay with you two?" Mrs. Palmer asked, and both Calvin and I nodded.

Calvin stood up then, so I did, too, and thanked his parents for the yummy dinner. I started to pick up my plate to take to the kitchen, but Mrs. Palmer said not to. "You're our guest. You don't need to clean up."

"So I guess we can go to my room?" Calvin asked, and then we both stared at each other for a few awkward seconds until Chelsea saved us.

"Ana, I'm so glad you brought your dog over. Pancake has been moping since I've been home. Look at this." She held out her phone to show me a picture of Pancake sitting inside a furry boot, looking up at the camera with huge eyes. "See? She's been hiding. In my Ugg boots!"

I looked over at Calvin. "You don't mean . . ."

"Don't say it . . ."

"I have to! I mean it's a pug. In an Ugg."

"And it's on a rug!"

Chelsea rolled her eyes at us. "You two are a perfect pair. Ana, it was great to meet you. I've got to do some studying. You guys be good." Chelsea disappeared into her room. I caught a glimpse of it—she had a patterned bedspread, with brightly colored throw pillows and a swath of fabric hanging on the wall.

I followed Calvin down the hall and into his room. It was bigger than the one I shared with Tali.

"Pancake had been hiding in my closet most of the time, until Chels got back with her boot collection. She likes to hide right there." Calvin pointed to the floor of his small closet. "Pancake, not Chelsea, that is. Sorry about the misplaced modifier."

"It's okay, I think," I said with a laugh. "I'm not sure I know what that is."

"Our teacher last year was really strict about grammar," Calvin said. He looked a little embarrassed, so I decided not to ask him anything else about that. I knew how it felt when you nerded out in front of someone and then they made fun of you for it.

I looked around Calvin's room. Unlike his sister's room, which already looked like she lived there, Calvin's was almost completely blank. A row of boxes lined one wall—some were opened, but still had stuff in them. Some looked like they hadn't even been opened yet.

"I haven't really finished unpacking," Calvin said as he saw me looking at the boxes.

I felt sad for Calvin suddenly. His sister didn't even really live here—she had a dorm at college—but she'd still put her things into her room in this apartment. Why wouldn't Calvin unpack? Did he not like it here? Maybe it was more that he missed his home so much.

"How come?" I asked him, sitting down on a small stuffed chair beside his bed.

Calvin sat down on the floor across from me. First Pancake and then Osito sat down beside him, each pug resting a head on one of his legs.

Calvin sighed. "I guess Pancake's not the only one who's having trouble adjusting." He patted his pug. "Everything's just so *different* in New York. It's not that I don't like it, exactly, but sometimes it seems like I've . . . lost everything I had before. For one thing, I've always been so excited to get my driver's permit in high school, and eventually get a car. I *love* cars. But the other day my dad said that since we live in the city now, we won't need to bother with all that."

Calvin had been looking down at the dogs, petting each one, but now he looked up at me. "Maybe that sounds dumb . . ."

"No—not at all!" I said. "But you know, you could still get a car eventually. Lots of New Yorkers drive."

"Yeah, but it seems a lot scarier to learn up here than it did back home, that's for sure. All those swerving taxicabs and people crossing the street without waiting for the light to change!"

"That's true," I agreed. I didn't really know what to tell him. I realized at that moment that I'd never really considered a life outside New York—and I hadn't ever thought about whether or not I'd learn to drive. But my ultimate dream job was working for Google, and I knew their headquarters were in California. That idea, though, seemed a lifetime away. "Do you still have friends or relatives you could visit back in Florida? You could still learn there, at least at first," I suggested.

"Yeah, my grandparents on my dad's side are there. I guess you're right."

"You know, New York's not so bad," I told him. "In fact, a lot of people think it's the greatest city on earth. Maybe give it some more time? You can still explore the neighborhood on foot."

Calvin met my eyes and nodded. "I'm sure you're right. It also helps when Pancake's not so glum and wants to go out for walks instead of hiding in a closet or a boot. Hey, that reminds me, I saw a flyer in our building lobby about a dog Easter egg hunt next Friday. We have off school, I checked. I thought maybe we could take P and O."

My mind started racing for a way out. Even though I really wanted to go. A dog Easter egg hunt? How fun did that sound? But there was no way Mrs. R would understand why I was taking her dog for the whole day.

Unless I'd be taking Osito to the same event with *Phoebe's* imaginary dog.

"That sounds fun. I'll ask my parents," I heard myself saying.

"Great!"

I checked the time on my phone. "Hey, it's getting late. I should get going."

"Okay." Calvin moved and both dogs grumbled at being displaced. "Pancake and I will walk you guys."

"Thanks," I said.

"I'm going to walk Ana home," Calvin told his parents, who were watching TV in the living room.

"Not alone you're not," his mom said, and I wondered if maybe Calvin being worried about New York was coming from his mom, or maybe both his parents. "Dan, will you go . . . ?" she started asking his dad.

But then Chelsea appeared in the kitchen and rescued us again. "I'll go, Daddy. Felt like a walk anyway."

Mr. Palmer gave me some gelato in a little cup with a lid to take home, and he and Mrs. Palmer waved good-bye as Calvin and Chelsea and I got in the elevator with the dogs in tow.

"Mom and Dad aren't quite used to the city yet," Chelsea told me. "I'm probably the only one who thinks life here is normal, since I've been living in DC for two years."

"Is Tampa a really small city, then?" I asked them.

"We're rounding up when we say we're from Tampa," Chelsea said. "We lived in the suburbs, in Westchase."

Ah, I thought. Calvin was a suburban guy. Maybe I could help turn him into more of a city guy, though.

"Thanks for walking home with us," I told Chelsea as we strolled east on Ninth Street, Pancake and Osito happily sniffing the sidewalk. "I mean, it would've been sort of awkward if we'd had to walk with . . ."

"My dad," Calvin finished. "Yep, sometimes it's not so bad having a sister."

"I totally agree," I said. "Even though I have to share a room with mine."

"How old is she?" Chelsea asked.

"She's turning fifteen in three weeks. It's a huge birthday. Well, it is if you're Puerto Rican, like we are."

"Oh, she's having a *quinceañera*?" Chelsea asked. "Did I say that right?"

"You did, and yeah, she's having one. A massive one. It's like taking over our lives."

Chelsea grinned. "This girl in my high school had one, but I didn't get invited. I was jealous—she had the biggest party."

"Mom and Dad rented out an entire dance club for your sweet sixteen," Calvin reminded her.

"Yeah, but I had to wait a whole extra year!" Chelsea said with a laugh.

"Okay, this is my building right here," I said as we reached my front stoop. "Thanks again."

"It was great to meet you, Ana!" Chelsea said. "Hope to see you around again real soon." It didn't surprise me much when she wrapped me in another big hug.

Then it seemed weird, I guess, if Calvin didn't hug me, too, especially since I'd just *met* his sister, and he was my actual friend.

Calvin stepped forward and I did, too, and then we knocked our foreheads together with a loud *thwack*, and I stepped back, seeing spots and rubbing my forehead.

Ack.

"Maybe we'll hug later," Calvin said awkwardly, also rubbing his temple. Chelsea was pulling him away by the elbow and I could see she was trying not to laugh.

I picked up Osito and pulled open the door to our building. Our puppy playdate had gone pretty well, I thought. Right up until the head injury, that is.

9

Delicious Dog Eggs

"Anaaaaaa!!!"

I heard my mom yelling my name as I stepped inside our apartment. It was Wednesday afternoon, and already the week seemed to be taking forever. Mom had me running all over the neighborhood, picking up this or that for Tali's quince. I couldn't wait until Friday, when I had no school, and the doggy egg hunt to look forward to with Osito, Calvin, and Pancake.

I set down the stationery-store bag that was full of the place cards for the party, and glanced around the apartment. It was looking more and more like an episode of *Hoarders: Party Edition*.

I gave a huge sigh. At least in a little more than two weeks, the madness would be over.

"Yeah?" I called out to Mom.

"Come back here!" Her voice was muffled.

"Where's here?" I asked, heading toward my parents' bedroom. But when I stuck my head inside and called for her again, Mom's voice came from the room I shared with Tali.

"What is it?" I asked when I walked into the room.

"Well, hello to you, too." Mom poked her head out from my closet, which she'd clearly been ransacking.

"What's going on?" I asked, walking over to the closet and frowning at the mess Mom had made. I always liked to keep my clothes and shoes in careful order.

"I'm trying to find your dress for the quince—why don't I see it?"

I flopped down onto the edge of my bed. "Um, probably because it's mythical."

"What? Is that some slang term?"

"No, I mean, you don't see my dress because it doesn't exist."

She was staring at me with her mouth open, a shocked look

on her face. "No. We talked about you wearing the dress you wore to your cousin Rebeca's wedding."

I started laughing, and Mom's expression grew angry.

"I'm sorry, but Mom—I was *nine* when Rebeca got married. I don't know where that dress actually is, but it doesn't matter, 'cause it's definitely not gonna fit."

"Nine?" she echoed. "But I could swear . . . we talked about you wearing it . . ."

I shook my head. "It must have been a conversation you planned to have."

"I do that sometimes, I know." Mom sat down on the edge of Tali's bed. "So what you're saying is, you need a new dress?"

I felt another bubble of laughter well up as I imagined myself wearing the tiny white dress I'd worn so long ago. I stifled the giggle. "I guess I do."

"Okay. I get off early on Friday. We can go shopping then."

"I can't this Friday. I'm taking Osito to that egg hunt, remember? I asked you and Papi the other day."

Mom frowned again. "Ana, that's the only time I have. We really need to get you that dress. I need to check it off my list."

I stood up, feeling the heat climb my neck like small flames. "I'm so glad that I'm just an item you have to check off your list," I huffed. "I really want to go to the egg hunt. We have school off that day. Can't I please do something that's actually fun for me for once? Instead of everything always being about Tali's party, twenty-four three-sixty-five?"

I watched the anger that had been starting to show on Mom's face get replaced with something else. Maybe guilt. "Okay," she said stiffly after a moment. "What time is that event?"

"It's at one."

"Well, how about you come back here by three and we'll still have a couple of hours to find your dress before I need to start dinner. Deal?"

"Okay," I said. And then it got awkward, since I kind of wanted to walk out of the room to end the conversation, but it was my room, and Mom didn't leave.

"I guess I'll put these clothes back." She looked around at the things she'd pulled down from my closet in search of the mythical dress.

"I can do it," I said. Mom nodded, and then she did leave.

I put away and reorganized my clothes, then collapsed back down on my bed. My phone buzzed and I saw that Calvin had texted me another photo of a pug. This one was of a puppy pug taking a bath. I giggled out loud and then started scrolling to find one to send back to him.

Without warning, Mom popped her head back into my room. "What about your escort?" she asked me. "Did you call Luis? You know, that friend of your cousin Tomas? I thought you called him already, but maybe I imagined that, too."

The phone call to Luis.

I felt a shudder go through me at the humiliating memory. "Nope. That actually happened. I called him yesterday after-noon, remember?"

"Oh right. Great," Mom said, and left me alone again.

I lay back down on my bed and groaned. There were so many rules about the *quinceañera*. I was trying to follow them, for Tali, even though the whole thing caused me major stress.

For example, the quince girl had to have fourteen *damas*, which were sort of like bridesmaids, and each *dama* needed to have a *chambelán*: an escort. Which meant that I had to call up a boy I didn't even know. My cousin Tomas had texted me his friend Luis's number, and somehow I'd worked up the nerve to make the call yesterday.

With trembling hands, I'd dialed the number and the line rang about fourteen times. I was about to hang up when a boy finally answered. Right away it was clear he was a major mumbler. I introduced myself and explained that I was Tomas's cousin Ana. Tomas had said Luis would be expecting to hear from me.

But all Luis said was:

"Yeahuh."

I continued, explaining about Tali's quince, and how I was a *dama* and needed an escort, and his reply was:

"Yeahuh."

"So," I went on, "I was hoping that since Tomas is coming as Tali's friend Linda's escort, you could just come along with him, and then if you ever need anybody for quince duty in the future you can totally call me—how does that sound?"

Luis: "Guesso."

And that had been that. I'd thanked him and hung up,

cringing at the awkwardness of it all. I'd immediately called Phoebe and told her the whole awful story.

"Ouch," Phoebe had said. "You sure you even want to go with this guy?"

"It's a giant pink party that I have to wear a fluffy dress to! I don't want to go at all. But the guy said yes. I think. That's good enough for me."

I blinked, coming out of the memories of yesterday. Then I looked down at my phone. I realized that while I'd been remembering my escort trauma, I'd been searching for a pug GIF. It probably looked to Calvin like I was typing a text this whole time. I quickly picked a pug wearing a hat with rabbit ears and sent it.

"Just a few more weeks," I said to myself out loud. "You can make it."

On Friday, Osito and I walked to the dog park to meet Calvin and Pancake. The doggy Easter egg hunt was being held at another park a few blocks away. Thankfully, Mrs. R had bought my story about going to the egg hunt with "Phoebe's dog." But I'd still felt an enormous wave of guilt as she'd said good-bye to us and I walked out the door with Osito.

When we arrived at the park, I sat on a bench with Osito on my lap, since I didn't want him to get too tired out before the hunt.

"Hey!" Calvin called, trotting over with Pancake. "You weren't waiting long, were you?"

"No, we're just chilling. I was early."

"Oh, good. It took me a few minutes to convince Pancake here to come out from under my bed." He said the last part with a frown, but then I watched him paste on his usual smile to replace it. "Ready to head out?"

I stood up. "Yep, let's go."

We walked out of the park, with Calvin in the lead. "Hey, it's the other way," I called. "We're heading southwest toward Seward Park."

Calvin shook his head. "I don't know why I was leading the way. I barely know my way around the neighborhood. Still!"

"You'll get there!" I assured him. "You just moved here. You know, there are people who've lived in one neighborhood their whole lives and they don't even know how to navigate the rest of the city."

"I definitely don't want to be one of those people," Calvin said. "I always want to know, just, like *more* about everything, you know? Like Pancake here—my aunt got her for me as a Christmas present two years ago, and then I read everything I could about pugs. My mom told me it was probably a good thing, since these guys need special care. I mean, cleaning the folds is a bear all by itself."

"Yeah," I echoed, "totally." I looked down at the little bear in my arms. I wasn't quite sure what Calvin was talking about—and then a few seconds later I realized that he meant cleaning underneath the folds of skin on pugs' faces. I'd never washed Osito—or any pug—before. I wondered if Mrs. R was keeping up with cleaning Osito's face—I knew she'd been having more and more trouble with her back lately. I decided to check once I brought Osito to her place.

We'd been walking along at Pancake's pace, but now Calvin picked her up. "You're probably smart to carry Osito the whole way," he said. "It's easy to forget how little walking they can do. Chelsea threatened to get me a stroller for walking Pancake in the city."

"I've seen little dogs in strollers around," I said. "I have to say, I think that would be adorable."

"That's what I'm afraid of," Calvin said in a dry voice, and I laughed.

When we reached Seward Park I looked up and saw the banner for the THIRD ANNUAL DOG EASTER EGG HUNT. We walked up to a table set up just inside the park.

"Do you have tickets?" a woman wearing pink denim overalls asked us, and I started to say no.

But then Calvin took out his phone, opened his email, and the woman scanned the tickets there.

"I didn't know you needed tickets," I said. "How much do I owe you?"

Calvin gave me a look I couldn't quite figure out. "You don't owe me anything. I'm just happy that you came with me."

"Oh. Of course. I mean, I'm happy, too. To be here, I mean."

What was wrong with me? Suddenly I was really bad at talking.

"Okay, so here are the dogs' numbers," the woman said, handing us each a kerchief. "They have to wear these in the hunt. There's a prize for the dog that finds the most eggs."

I looked over at a huge Labrador retriever nearby. "I don't think our little pugs stand too much of a chance," I whispered to Calvin.

"Well, there's a winner in both the small and large dog categories. But I'm thinking ours are still at a disadvantage." Calvin pointed to a Jack Russell terrier. "Really athletic and energetic breeds like that have a serious advantage. But at least pugs have one thing going for them—they're pretty food motivated."

"Why would that matter?" I asked.

"That's how the dogs find the eggs. They've got meaty snacks inside."

"Sounds delicious."

Calvin laughed and bent down to put Pancake's kerchief around her neck. I did the same with Osito, then looked around and saw that some of the dog owners had gone all out. There were dogs wearing Easter or spring-themed T-shirts, dogs with bunny ears on their heads, and some of the owners were dressed up, too. "I think we missed out on the costume part," I said.

"Next year," Calvin said, which made me smile. That meant Calvin thought we'd still be hanging out next year—and maybe I'd also have my own dog by then, not a borrowed one. I felt yet another flash of guilt.

We followed the direction everyone was moving in, and we got to the little area that had been fenced in for the small dogs. A voice called out that the hunt had begun, so we let Osito and Pancake off their leashes and watched the two of them waddle off together, noses to the ground. Osito started sniffing around some shrubs, and I bent down to look. I saw a flash of bright green on the ground, then picked up the egg.

"Good boy!" I told Osito, and he barked.

As I was feeding him the treat inside, there was a rustle in the bushes. A ridge of fur stood up on Pancake's back, and in a flash she started running, following what I saw now was a squirrel. I grabbed Osito, and followed Calvin as he ran after Pancake. The area was fenced in, but there must have been a hole, because

Pancake broke right through, and in another couple of seconds she was gone from our view. Calvin whirled around with a panicked expression.

"You go that way, I'll go this way," I said, pointing, and Calvin nodded.

I clasped Osito tight against me as I ran. My heart was pounding so hard it made me feel sick. I couldn't believe Pancake had gotten away from us. It had all happened so fast.

Just one thought echoed in my head as I ran:

We *had* to find Pancake. We had to.

10
Lost

I ran, calling Pancake's name, for four or five blocks. I was starting to really panic. Calvin had gone in one direction, and I'd gone
in another, but what if Pancake had gone straight ahead, or dou-
bled back through the park somehow? Plus, running around
carrying Osito wasn't easy. He only weighed ten pounds or so, but
he seemed to be getting heavier. And I could tell he was upset—
he was picking up on my stress, and he'd started to whimper.

I forced myself to stop. Then I did what I always did when I
needed backup—I called my best friend and my sister. I dialed
Phoebe first and then had her add Tali to the call.

"Pancake ran away from Calvin and me," I said without pre-amble. "Can either of you come help? I'm trying to carry Osito, and I don't know how far Calvin went—we ran in different directions."

"Where are you?" Phoebe asked.

"Pancake ran away at Seward Park. I ran over to Orchard Street—on the Canal Street side. I sent Calvin toward Grand Street, but I don't know . . ."

"I can bike over there," Phoebe said. "We'll meet back up at the park. I'm leaving now," she said, and clicked off the call.

"I'm close, too," Tali said. "I'm at the noodle shop on East Broadway with Ella and Haley. Hold on and I'll ask if either of them can come help." I heard some muffled words and then Tali came back on the line. "They can both come," she said. "We'll be there in a couple of minutes."

"Thank you, thank you!" I said, and breathed a sigh of relief. I was about to call Calvin when my phone rang—it was him.

"Ana," he said. "I can't find her, and I don't even know where *I* am now. What am I gonna do?" It sounded a little like he might be about to cry.

"We'll find her," I said. "Phoebe is coming, plus my sister and her two friends. They'll all be here really soon. We'll cover all the directions."

"But she could have gone anywhere." His voice broke on the word *anywhere*, and my heart broke along with it.

"We'll find her," I repeated. "Right now we just need to get you back to the park. Go into your map app and just type in Seward Park. Make sure you hit the little person icon for walking directions. Do you want me to stay on the line with you? I will, but I can probably keep watch for Pancake better if . . ."

"No. I'll call back if I have trouble with the directions. I'll see you at the park."

I could hear in his voice that Calvin was doing that thing he always did, which was to put on a brave front. I hung up, stuffed the phone in my back pocket, shifted little Osito to my other arm, and then started walking, keeping my eyes peeled for a flash of light brown fur. I thought about how Calvin and I had joked about a dog stroller, but right then I really wished I had one for Osito.

Suddenly I spotted a teenage girl holding a tan-colored dog, but when I caught up to her I felt a hot stab of disappointment. She was holding what turned out to be an oddly big Chihuahua.

When I got back to the park and saw the egg hunt was still going on I felt a flash of annoyance. How dare they just keep going after their crappy fencing-in job had led to Pancake getting out? I hadn't even let myself think about what could happen to her on this crowded, sunny Friday afternoon in the city. I thought of her running into the street, alone and scared, and then . . .

I closed my eyes for a second, as though it would stop the frightening images that were appearing in my mind.

"Hey. So what did the people say?" Phoebe was standing beside me.

I blinked in surprise. "The people . . . ?"

"Running this event. You mean you didn't ask . . . ?"

At my look of confusion, Phoebe took off toward the registration table. A few moments later she was standing up on one of their chairs, holding a megaphone. "Attention. Can I get everybody's attention, please? We have a missing dog! She's a tan-colored pug, answers to the name of Pancake. Can everybody please stop looking for eggs right now and start looking for this missing pug instead? There's a . . . fifty-dollar reward for the person who finds her."

I stood shaking my head as I looked up at Phoebe. "You're a genius," I said when she jumped down and walked back over to me. "Why didn't I think of doing that?"

"Because you're upset," Phoebe said. "It's tough to think straight when you're upset. That's why I'm here."

"Thanks," I said, giving my bestie a hug.

"So, hey," she added, "I said fifty because I figured we could probably scrape that together, but do you think Calvin would offer more? It might make people more motivated."

Just then Calvin appeared, out of breath and wild-eyed. "Hey," he said to Phoebe.

"I've got everyone at the egg hunt looking for Pancake," she told him. "I offered a fifty-dollar reward; hope that's okay? But I was just saying to Ana how we could offer more maybe . . ."

"Of course!" Calvin's face changed into an almost smile. "That's brilliant; why didn't we think of that? Offer a hundred— two hundred! I'll call my dad and get him to bring . . ."

"I think a hundred will work just fine as a carrot," Phoebe

said, and went back over to the table. One of the organizers got up and made another announcement that the finder's fee was now one hundred dollars, and she said that the pug might be outside the park.

The same woman came over to us then and told Calvin how sorry she was about his dog getting out. An older man with a white beard came up to us and offered to give Calvin *his* dog for one hundred dollars.

"Thanks. We're looking for the one specific dog," Phoebe told the man.

Tali spotted us and waved, and she and her friends Ella and Haley came over to us. I explained what Phoebe had done and suggested we all keep looking.

"I think we should cover the perimeter of the park," I said, and Tali nodded.

"I'm so sorry about your dog," Haley said to Calvin.

I kind of wanted to yell at her not to say that, since we were *going* to find Pancake.

"Haley and Ella, how about you guys take the Broadway and Canal side of the park? Tali, you head over toward the library."

Phoebe was talking very fast, as usual, but for once I didn't mind. "Ana and I can cover Hester Street. Calvin, I think you should stay here in case someone finds her."

Calvin nodded, looking grateful. "My dad's on his way with reward money—should I send him somewhere to look when he gets here?"

"I think he should just wait with you," Tali told him.

"Will you hold Osito while I search, then?" I asked Calvin. "I hate to ask, but he's getting really heavy . . ."

"It's okay. Sure." He accepted the dog from my arms.

"Maybe have your dad talk to the event people," Phoebe suggested. "Adults are always more helpful to other adults."

"And have him say their fence was broken!" I added as I started to follow Phoebe. I turned back to Calvin. "Will you be okay?"

He nodded once. Clearly, he wasn't okay, but I knew that the only thing that would really help would be finding Pancake.

Phoebe and I looked all around the park on our way out. Once we stepped out of the park, I started calling Pancake's name and Phoebe joined in. Calvin's creative name for his dog made it seem a little weird, I decided, since now my best friend and I were walking down the sidewalk yelling "Pancake!" and everybody kept giving us strange looks. Phoebe asked passersby if they'd seen a pug. Everyone either ignored her or shook their heads.

I couldn't shake the feeling that we were missing something—that maybe there was some other way to find Pancake. And then I thought of the treats that had been inside the dog eggs. What if Pancake hadn't gone all that far after she chased the squirrel? What if she was crouched down hiding somewhere, just out of sight in the bushes, too scared to come out? Maybe, though, if she smelled treats . . .

"Just stay here for one minute while I run back into the park, okay?" I asked Phoebe, and she nodded.

I ran up to the registration table. "Hi," I said to the woman in overalls. "I'm trying to find the missing pug? Can you give me some of the treats like you had inside the eggs? If she's hiding, maybe the dog would come out for treats."

"We have a bunch of kinds, but these are my dog's favorite," the woman said as she handed me a small bag. "Good luck."

I ran back to Phoebe and handed her some treats out of the bag. Then I shook some into my hand. "Let's see if we can try to lure her out," I said.

I crouched low and held out my hand near the bushes. I hoped that no bold city squirrels would come steal the treats. Squirrels, I figured, had caused enough trouble for one day. I continued to call Pancake's name more softy. Nothing.

I was about to stand up when I heard a small whimper. And then I saw what looked like a swath of tan fur.

I moved closer, and saw first an ear, then a flat pug face. It was Pancake! I'd found her! I felt a rush of relief.

Moving carefully, so as not to frighten her, I picked her up. She ate the treats out of my hand and snuggled closer to me. Her tiny heart was pounding so loud. She was dirty, but other than that she looked okay.

"Phoebe!" I yelled. "I found her!"

When Phoebe reached me, I had her call Tali and tell her to stop looking. "Do you want me to call Calvin?" Phoebe asked.

"We're almost back to where he is," I said. "Let's just let him see."

Calvin's back was to me when we walked into the park, so I called his name.

His face when he saw that I was holding Pancake went from relief to joy to falling apart in the space of just a few seconds. I handed her to him; Pancake was trembling just a little bit, but she went crazy with happiness when she got to Calvin. She started licking his face, and he was laughing. I saw that Mr. Palmer had gotten there, and he patted his son on the back and swiped once at his eyes. Calvin wasn't crying now, but it looked like maybe he had while we'd been searching for his dog. I didn't blame him at all.

Mr. Palmer was holding Osito's leash and the little bear was dancing around Calvin's legs. I picked him up and right away he started trying to claw his way out of my arms, which he'd never done before. After a few seconds I decided that maybe he was trying to get closer to Pancake. I stepped closer to Calvin, and my suspicions were confirmed as Osito started licking his new friend all over her face.

"Aww," I said.

"I think he was worried, too," Calvin said.

When Osito had finished licking Pancake's face, I pulled him close to my chest and looked into his wise, dark eyes. His soft, furry body felt solid against mine. For a few seconds I didn't think about anything else except for how much I loved him, and how much I would miss him if he weren't there.

Calvin looked over at me. "Thank you, Ana," he said. Ella, Haley, Tali, and Phoebe were crowded around him now, petting Pancake's head and cooing at her.

I shook my head. "I didn't do anything—just got lucky and found her."

"I saw you go get those treats. That was a really good idea."

"Phoebe's idea was better—about the reward."

"Oh! I brought the reward," Calvin's dad said, reaching for his wallet.

I put a hand up. "No! That was for if a stranger found her."

Mr. Palmer smiled. "Of course. But you're still going to be regarded as a hero in our family for all time. In fact, you've got to come over for pizza this week. I bought a new stone for the oven, and I think I've perfected the crust. I'll put it up against any New York pizza."

Calvin grinned. "Yes, you—and Osito—have to come soon. To hang out with me . . . and Pancake," he said.

I saw Tali give me a curious look. But the sight of Tali made me remember something I'd forgotten in all the chaos of losing Pancake.

I pulled my phone out to check the time. Five minutes after four. I was over an hour late for dress shopping with Mom.

"I was supposed to meet Mom at three!" I cried, turning to Tali. "To find a dress."

"We gotta go," Tali told everyone, and before I'd had time to say anything else to Calvin, or do more than wave to Phoebe, we were on our way out of the park and headed home.

I looked down at Osito, who'd been carried at top speed more today than probably anytime in his doggy life. I thought he gave me a long-suffering look.

"Just be glad you're not a human," I told him. "It's really very complicated."

11

The Ruffle Monster

I was afraid of being grounded, but it turned out my actual punishment was worse: Since I'd missed meeting Mom at the store, she'd gone ahead and picked out a dress for me. It was very white, very ruffled, and Mom proudly held it up as soon as I walked in our front door with Tali. My sister had, helpfully, already called Mom to explain that my friend's dog had gone missing so we'd all needed to pitch in and that's why I hadn't made it to the store. Mom wasn't even mad. She was just focused on the dress.

"Isn't it perfect?" she asked me.

"It's very . . . ruffly."

"I know, so pretty!" Mom said. She bustled ahead to my room and I followed her, watching as she hung the dress on the back of my closet door.

"Now try it on!" Mom ordered.

My only hope was that it wouldn't fit, but Mom had done her homework and checked the size of the dress I'd worn for Christmas just a few months ago. I stepped into the dress and Tali zipped me up. It fit like a glove. A very white, very ruffly glove.

"Wonderful!" Mom said, clapping her hands. She left the room, clearly pleased that she could check this item off her endless list.

Still wearing the Ruffle Monster, as I had already named it, I turned to Tali. "I like how on Wednesday she thinks I'm nine years old, but today she can buy my exact size no problem."

"Sorry, sis," Tali said, sitting on her bed and checking her phone.

I got changed back into my normal clothes and then hung

the Ruffle Monster back up onto my closet door. I snapped a shot of it to send to Phoebe. She responded immediately with the crying-while-laughing-face emoji, and then in all caps:

GET THE SCISSORS.

I laughed and typed back:

If I cut up this dress Mom will END me

Phoebe texted back:

Lol not 2 destroy it—maybe we can de-ruffle?!?

"Phoebe says we should de-ruffle it," I told Tali.

"Geez, that's a scary idea I want no part of." Tali walked over to where I'd hung it on the front of my closet door. "I mean, it's not *that* bad."

A loud snort was my only response.

"Okay, it's not great."

I flopped back onto my bed with a sigh. "I guess that's what I get for not meeting Mom at the store and picking out my own dress. But if I had to choose between finding Pancake and this dress, I'd wear this dress for a month. Today could have been so much worse." I sat up. "Just remind me I said that when I actually have to wear the dress, yeah?"

"I will," Tali promised. "Though I'd pay real money to see you wear it for a month."

School on Monday felt almost like a relief. I was anxious to get away from the party preparations, which were reaching a fever pitch—not to mention the Ruffle Monster just hanging there in our small room. Mocking me.

In coding class, though, Ms. Vasquez passed out the scoring rubric for our big project, and I felt a flood of panic. Usually I would have a project like this halfway done, at least. After all, it counted for 20 percent of our grade.

I didn't really have an excuse. Ms. V had announced the project at the beginning of the semester. I'd thought of a few different ideas, but none of them seemed perfect. But now, I knew, I was just going to have to pick one and start coding the site. In addition to creating a working website, we also had to give a presentation to the class using multimedia. I was counting on Phoebe to help direct a video presentation for me. But first, I had to have a concept, and a script, and all the rest.

Ms. Vasquez told us we were going to have the rest of the class period to work, and Calvin turned to me.

"What's your project going to be about?" he asked.

"I'm not sure yet," I said. I realized that I'd been so distracted by Calvin and Osito and Pancake, and getting tripped up in more and more complicated lies *about* Osito, that I hadn't been focusing as much on school as I usually did.

"How was the rest of your weekend?" I asked Calvin as I logged in to my computer. "I bet you didn't let Pancake out of your sight."

"You're right. I stayed home with her the whole time. I only left to go to my aunt's house on Sunday. I thought about bringing her, but I felt like she was safer at home."

"Osito and I missed you at the park," I said.

"I'm still a little freaked out after the escape, I guess," he said. "But, hey, I wanted to just say, I mean—thank you again for finding her. I can't even explain how much I . . ."

"You don't have to thank me, or say anything like that," I told him, trying to spare us any embarrassment.

"Has Osito ever run off on you? My mom said that every dog runs away from their owner at some point or other. But maybe she was just trying to make me feel better."

I felt the next lie bubbling up in my brain right away. "Oh, sure, he ran once, when he was younger. He's crazy about squirrels. You know how much trouble those darn squirrels can be," I added.

"That's weird. He didn't even seem to notice the one in the park that Pancake ended up chasing. He was just standing there stock still, and then you picked him up."

Oh man, Calvin was right. Osito clearly wasn't *crazy* about squirrels. "Nah, that was just my lightning reflexes," I lied some more. "I knew he *would* have chased it, but I can't help it. I'm basically a ninja."

Calvin was looking at me like he was trying to see the hidden ninja. "Okay. I'll have to watch out for that side of you."

"So what's your project going to be about?" I asked quickly, hoping for a change of subject.

"I'm thinking of doing something like tips for new New Yorkers. You know, like a site for people who just moved here? I figure I can use all the advice I gather for myself, too, especially after Friday."

"What do you mean?"

Calvin frowned for a second. "I was basically useless. I didn't know my way around. Or have any idea what to do."

"You're being too hard on yourself. I didn't know anything, either. I mean, I know the neighborhood, but I grew up here. Phoebe was the one who thought about offering the reward. She's really good at thinking fast like that."

"Oh, hey—where is Phoebe, by the way?" Calvin asked, looking around.

"Her grandparents are in town so she's absent today."

"Oh. So, you didn't tell me what your project was going to be about."

At Calvin's mention of Phoebe, I'd automatically checked my phone, to see if she'd texted. There was no text from Phoebe, but I did see my save screen, which was an adorable picture of Osito.

And that's when the kernel of an idea came to me.

"It's going to be a site for dog owners!" I declared, inspiration hitting me. "To help them with things they need. Like, people to help walk their dog when they can't." *Kind of like I do for Mrs. R and Osito*, I thought, but didn't add.

"Cool idea," Calvin said.

"I hope so," I said.

I needed to get my head back in the game. I had a lot riding on my GPA at the end of this year.

"Are you going to the park this afternoon?" Calvin asked.

"Yes. Are you going to bring Pancake?"

"I was thinking I should take her back. I have to get past the escape. But that was probably our last egg hunt."

"I get that."

The bell rang then and we both logged out of our computers and stood up. "So I'll see you later? Maybe you and Osito could come over for dinner?"

"I'm on kitchen duty," I heard myself lie. I barely even had to think about it. Was this what happened with lying—did it get easier? Was I getting *good* at it?

"Okay. But my dad wants to make you his pizza so we'll have to find a night that works."

"I'll ask tonight," I promised, already thinking of reasons that Osito might need to visit Phoebe's imaginary dog so I could get Mrs. R to let me take him out at night yet again.

12

Now You Have to Find Your Own Pink Guy

"My mom said to ask you about dog licenses," Calvin said when we met up later at the park. "Where do I go to get one? Pancake's still got hers from Westchase right now."

I felt the now-familiar rush of heated embarrassment that came along with getting tangled in my web of lies. I had no idea where to get dog licenses or if Osito had one.

My phone buzzed and I saw it was my sister calling.

"I should get this," I told Calvin. Tali almost always just texted, so I was worried.

"Hey, sis," Tali said. "So, the thing is, Mom just remembered about the piñata that got ruined. I was planning to not mention it—it seemed like maybe she forgot, which was one hundred percent okay by me. I don't need one at the party. But then she just remembered it, and she started getting all worked up, and I, well, I may have accidentally . . ."

"Tali," I broke in. "Just spit it out, okay?"

"Well, Mr. Levy can't special order another one this late. So, the thing is, I accidentally said you were going to get a new one. I said you already knew of a place."

"Tali!"

"I know, I know! But she started complaining about how you let the other one get ruined . . ."

"Yeah, how dare I do something so awful as get caught in a storm! Geez, sometimes I don't even understand what Mami wants from me."

"I know, sis. And that's why I jumped in and, well . . . lied and said you had a line on one. But do you think you could actually find one? I mean, you're such a whiz at web research."

I gave a sigh. "I'll find one. No biggie."

"I'm really sorry, Ana!" Tali said, and I could hear the wobble in her voice. My poor sister had just been trying to calm Mom down, but now she'd dragged me into the problem. "Mom's especially wound up today. Cousin Javier just came to stay for a couple days, which I think she totally forgot about, and it's all a mess . . ."

"Ugh, Javier?" I asked with a groan. Of all my many cousins, Javier was far and away my least favorite. Unfortunately, he was also the one who came to the city and stayed with us every few months to participate in his karate competitions.

"Yeah, he's here. And he keeps practicing 'his moves.' He's kind of just the worst," she added in a whisper.

I sighed.

"Will you be home soon?" Tali asked in a hopeful voice.

"On my way," I said with another sigh. I couldn't leave Tali alone with wound-up Mom, party madness . . . *and* Cousin Javier.

"Okay, sis. See you in a bit."

I hung up and turned to Calvin. "Sorry. Another party crisis."

"Sounded like it. What happened?"

"Do you remember that big bag I was carrying—in the storm, the day we met?" Calvin nodded. "Well, that was a piñata in there, and it kind of melted in all that rain."

"Oh, man—I'm sorry. That stinks. But I'm sure you can find another one. Don't they have everything in New York?"

I thought hard. "I don't know where to get one. That one was special order. It'd be really expensive to ship something so gigantic. And I've seen some places nearby that have them, but mostly they're like of cartoon cars and stuff. I need to find one that would fit in to my sister's party theme."

"What's the theme?"

"Princess Explosion," I said wryly, and Calvin laughed.

"Hey," he said. "I think I might actually know of a place— over by our new apartment. From the outside it looks like mainly a card store, but I swear I saw a pink piñata in the window, too. I can take a look on the way home and let you know tomorrow."

"Wow, thanks—that'd be great! See, you know stuff about the neighborhood that I don't already!"

Calvin smiled, but it wasn't a very convincing one. I knew he was still bothered about what had happened on Friday.

"Hey, I'm really sorry, but it sounds like my mom is in full panic mode—and I forgot my annoying cousin is visiting. I should head home. I'll see you at school tomorrow, okay?"

"Okay. See you tomorrow."

I realized as I left the park that I'd managed to get out of there before Calvin remembered to ask me where I'd gotten the license for my dog. Like Tali said, I was a pretty decent computer whiz. I was sure I could find the answer for him by tomorrow.

What a tangled web, Charlotte, said a voice in my head. It sounded a little like Phoebe's, but the voice sounded like my own, too.

"So your sister told you what you need to do?" Mom asked me at dinner that night. Cousin Javier was there, shoveling in Mom's *pasteles* like he'd never eaten food before. I rolled my eyes when I saw he was still wearing his stupid karate gi. Why couldn't he change into jeans like a normal person?

I nodded. "I think I have a lead on where to find one. Hopefully they'll have a pink one to match the theme."

Mom lowered the forkful of food she'd been about to eat. "A what? A pink *boy*? Is that some new slang or something?"

"I was talking about—wait, what are *you* talking about?" I looked over at Tali and she looked mighty guilty.

"I was going to tell you *that* part in person," my sister said, sinking down a little in her chair.

"You got stood up," Javier said around a mouthful of *pasteles*.

"Wait, *what*?" I cried. "You mean Tomas's friend isn't coming?"

Tali was starting to look even guiltier.

"That's what *stood up* means, genius," Javier put in.

"Nice robe, Javier," I snapped.

I groaned and closed my eyes to compose myself. The day after Tali's party I intended to tell my parents that I didn't want a party at all when I turned fifteen. I'd do the part at church, if they wanted, but no pink dress, no piñatas, and definitely no making my sister and cousins find *escorts*. How embarrassing.

I glared at Javier. "I did not get stood up. That guy has never even met me. But now I guess I need . . ."

"Now you have to find your own pink guy," Javier said with a smirk, and I threw a slice of tomato at him.

"Ana! Honestly, since when do you throw food at the table? It's like this family has all gone crazy," Mom exclaimed.

"Yeah, how rude," Javier added with a snicker.

Papi raised his eyes from his plate to give him a look. "Ana, please don't worry about finding an escort. It will all be fine," Papi said in his calm voice. Our father was always the reasonable one in the family.

I sighed. "I still can't wait until this party's over." I'd just been venting my frustration about the escort situation, but when I met my sister's wounded eyes, I felt like a jerk.

I tried to tell her I was sorry, but for the rest of the meal she didn't raise her head from her plate, and a few minutes later she asked to be excused. I took one more bite and did the same.

Once back in our shared room, my apology burst out of me. "Oh, Tali—I'm so sorry—I didn't mean to say that! It's just, there's so much going on, and you know how much Javier annoys me."

Tali sat down at her tiny desk. She didn't look up at me right away. "It's okay, Ana. I know my party's thrown the whole family into uproar."

"No, it's not so bad. I should never have said . . ."

Finally, my sister looked up at me. She gave me a weak smile. "I'm not mad, really. *I'm* sorry I didn't tell you about Luis backing out of being your escort. I was going to tell you when you got home. But I was thinking this was actually the perfect thing to happen. Now you can invite . . ."

"Don't say it." I cut her off. "I can't invite Calvin."

Tali gave me a puzzled frown. "Why not?"

I sat down on the edge of my bed. "Everything is already so confusing with Calvin, especially with all the lying and everything . . ."

"Lying? What did he lie about?"

Hearing my sister assume it was the other person who'd been lying made me feel like I'd just grown smaller. "It was me. I've been lying. He thinks Osito is my dog."

Tali stared at me thoughtfully for a few seconds. "Did he assume it and then you didn't correct him?"

"Yes, that's how it started. But it's been weeks, and I still haven't told him."

"Why not?"

"I'm not completely sure. At first, I was embarrassed, because I'd waited a little too long and it would have been weird. And then he started telling me about how Pancake was sort of depressed since they moved here, and the only time she acted like her old self was when Osito was around. And Osito has also been so much happier being with Pancake. So then I was afraid Calvin wouldn't want to hang around with me after I'd sort of lied, or that he wouldn't want his dog to hang out with my *neighbor's* dog. But it really seemed like he and Pancake both sort of . . . needed us."

Tali nodded. "I get that. But now you two are really friends, I think. You could tell him and he'd forgive you, I'm sure."

"Maybe. I don't know."

"Well, I think you should tell him. *And* you should ask him to be your *chambelán*."

Tali made it sound so easy. For Tali, finding an escort to her party had been as easy as asking the cutest boy at her school, who'd immediately said yes, of course. But even without all my lies about Osito, the thought of asking Calvin seemed pretty nerve-racking.

It had been hard enough to find Luis; Mom had put out the word through all our cousins, searching the five boroughs—and New Jersey—to find someone to take me. And now that Plan A had fallen through, we'd have to start the whole thing again.

Hmm. Maybe in that sense it *wouldn't* be so bad to ask Calvin. At least, unlike Luis, he didn't mumble. He *was* kind of—okay, very—cute. And I knew him already. He wouldn't be some stranger friend-of-a-friend-of-a-cousin. As long as I worked up the nerve . . .

"I guess I can ask him," I said to Tali.

She shrieked and stood up to hug me.

I was glad my sister was happy, but I was stressed. Not only did I have to find another piñata tomorrow, but I had to ask another boy to the quince. At least only one of those things actually needed to be pink.

WEBSITE DESIGN IDEAS

IDEA #3:

Chambelán locator.

Functions: Searchable database of boys willing to wear a tuxedo and serve as an escort to a *quinceañera*, for a small fee.

Searchable by: Location, those who own their own tux.

Goal: Avoid the embarrassing fate of being a *dama* without an escort.

Working-title ideas:

Shame-Free *Chambeláns*

Quince Nightmare-Avoider

So You Don't Have an Escort?

13

Absolutely Attached to Alliteration

On the way to the park the next afternoon, I rehearsed in my head what I would say to Calvin about the quince. When I'd seen him at school earlier, I'd chickened out—my specialty—and decided that I'd feel more comfortable when it was just us and the pugs.

I tried out some openings in my head:

Hey, Calvin, you're my friend. Friends do favors for friends, so, I need one . . .

Terrible.

So, Calvin, I have this embarrassing problem . . .

Definitely not *that*.

Calvin. You're a history person. Do you know the history of the quinceañera *celebration? I'll send you a link to the Wikipedia page! And then maybe you'll want to witness one for yourself? Because, coincidence: I can help with that!*

"Ugh, what's wrong with me?" I said aloud.

Osito looked up at me as if he was wondering the same thing.

We reached the gates to the dog run, and I opened them and stepped through. I breathed a sigh of relief, or maybe disappointment, when I didn't see Calvin among the dog owners or Pancake among the dogs.

I let Osito off his leash and sat down on one of the benches.

What if I just *didn't* ask Calvin at all? I'd panicked when I found out about Luis canceling, and then I'd let Tali talk me into this idea. But I could just turn the problem over to Phoebe. Maybe she could find some other guy to strong-arm into going with me.

Going with Calvin would be so much more complicated. I decided then and there to just forget the whole crazy plan.

Then I looked up and saw Calvin and Pancake coming through the gates. Calvin was carrying a big plastic bag that reminded me of the one I'd been stuck with on the day of the huge rainstorm. The day we met.

Calvin bent down to let Pancake loose. Pancake and Osito immediately ran to each other like they were the leads in a romantic movie, and I chuckled to see their happy reunion. Calvin walked over with a smile.

"Hey. How's it going?" Calvin asked, sitting down beside me on the bench.

"Not bad. What have you got there?"

"This is for you, actually," Calvin said, holding up the bag. "I went by that party store near my house and they *did* have a pink piñata just sitting there in the window. So I grabbed it for you."

"Seriously? That's so nice of you!" I felt my stomach jump at Calvin's sweet gesture. I peered down into the bag and saw it was indeed a big pink piñata, shaped like a star. "I don't have any money with me but I'll bring some tomorrow. How much was it?"

Calvin waved a hand. "It was twenty, but it's no big deal."

"I'll bring it." Calvin's kindness, the fact that he'd gone to the trouble, suddenly brought out my bravery. "Hey, speaking of my sister's party . . . ," I began, speaking quickly before I lost my nerve. "I hate to ask for another favor right now, but . . . are you free the Saturday after next?"

"Pretty sure I am, why?"

And just like that, my plan to *forget* the plan to ask Calvin was scrapped.

"So with a *quinceañera*, one of the traditions is that she has to have fourteen *damas*—like attendants . . . who all have to have escorts. Boys that go with them," I explained nervously. "And, well, the boy who was supposed to go with me, this friend of my cousin . . . he fell through. So I was wondering if maybe . . . would you be willing to come with me to—to fill in?"

Ack. I'd done it! I'd asked Calvin to accompany me to the party!

Was this a date? No. No. Of course not.

Calvin paused for what felt like forever. He was looking at me like he was trying to figure something out. I glanced over nervously at Osito and Pancake. They were happily racing around the dog run, playing with some of the other dogs, too.

Finally, Calvin spoke up. "I can fill in," he said. "What do I need to wear?"

"A tuxedo, actually . . . " Oh, man, I'd forgotten about the stupid tuxedo tradition. Now maybe he'd want to take back his yes. How could I ask him to go and rent a tux? But it'd be super weird if I offered to pay for it . . .

Calvin's voice broke through my stress spiral. "No problem. I have a tux. My mom always has to go to fancy events for her job, and sometimes the whole family has to go, too."

I stared at Calvin in disbelief. Could he even be real?

"That's . . . great!" I exhaled in happy relief. "Are you sure you don't mind . . . ?"

"Ana, I don't mind. I'm actually interested in seeing a real-life *quinceañera*."

I nodded, doubly relieved. "I'm glad."

"Should I bring a present for your sister?" Calvin asked.

"Nope. There will be a ton of food, though, so bring your appetite."

"That, I can do. Oh, hey, I almost forgot—I found this really funny video I wanted to show you."

Calvin scooted a little closer to me and tilted his phone to show me the video. He was so close our legs were almost touching.

Calvin was watching the clip and laughing, but I had trouble focusing on the pug in the video. Instead, I was thinking about Calvin, and sitting close to Calvin. I'd never been one of those girls to go all goopy and silly over a boy before. Phoebe and I were always laughing at the girls in our class who did. But something about this boy made me worry that I was starting down the goopy/silly path.

"I have to get back home," I told Calvin when the video ended. "It's my cousin's last night here and we're going out to dinner." I stood up and started trying to wrangle Osito back into his harness, but Pancake kept getting in the way.

"These two," I said.

"I know, right?" Calvin laughed.

I headed toward the gate with Osito, who whimpered back at Pancake.

"See you at school tomorrow," I told Calvin. "Thank you again so much for this," I added, lifting up the piñata bag. "And for agreeing to come to the quince."

"Sure thing," Calvin said.

For some reason I turned around one more time as I was leaving the park, and I saw that Calvin was still there, and it seemed like he was still looking in my direction. I waved at him and then turned to leave the park.

I had an escort. And a piñata. Quince problems solved!

As I walked home, I thought about the quince, when Calvin would meet Tali and my parents and the rest of my family. That made me nervous, and then I had a realization that made me *extra* nervous.

Calvin thought I had a dog. My family knew I did not have a dog.

Now I had a whole new set of quince problems.

"How about Puppy Pals?"

Phoebe gave a loud groan and crumpled up her sandwich wrapper. "Terrible. What else you got?"

"Walking Warriors?" I offered.

"That sounds like people will be doing battle with the dogs. Why are you so stuck on alliteration?"

I sat back in my chair at our lunch table. "I don't know. I just am."

Today was the day I was getting serious about my coding project. I'd actually gotten excited about the idea I'd had while talking to Calvin—creating a website for people like Mrs. R who needed help with their dogs. The best part was that Phoebe, my ace video director, had already come up with a great idea for the presentation. Instead of me standing there explaining the website, there'd be Osito looking cute up on the video, and I would do the voice-over.

"You *should* have the word *walking* or *walkers* in there some-where," Phoebe said. "Since that's the service the website will provide, right? Connecting people with dogs to people who will walk dogs. Like you and Mrs. Ramirez."

"Yeah. But then I have to get the *dog* part in, too. What dog words start with *w*?"

"Argh, you're obsessed with alliteration!" Phoebe laughed.

"Okay . . . hmm, this is hard. There aren't that many *w* words." She sipped from her milk and then her eyes grew big. "Oh, I got it! Woof!"

"Woof Walkers?"

"Okay, no. Sounds weird. Wag. Like a tail."

"Wag Walkers." Then inspiration struck. "Ooh—how about Waggle Walkers?"

Phoebe frowned. "What's a waggle?"

"I think it means the same thing as wag, like with a dog's tail." I typed the word into my phone. Yes! *Shake, flap, jiggle* were the synonyms that came up. "Waggle Walkers. I like the sound of that."

"It's pretty catchy, I'll admit." Phoebe grinned. "I mean, it's no Extreme Long Shot . . ."

"Your site name *is* awesome," I said. Phoebe's website was for kids who wanted to be filmmakers. I liked how the name was a pun—it was a type of camera shot, but it was also what almost everyone tells kids, Phoebe says, when they announce that they want to be filmmakers.

"But your site will win when it comes to functionality," Phoebe added. "My coding sucks."

"Your coding does not suck! Besides, I promised to help you if you needed it, since you're helping me with the video."

"Your video *will* be amazing," Phoebe assured me. "You done eating?"

I nodded, folding up my lunch bag. "Um, Phoebe? Before we go, I need help with one more thing. Calvin's coming to Tali's quince as my escort." I said those last words in an embarrassed rush.

Phoebe's eyes widened. "You asked him? Dang, girl, I'm impressed! Calvin will be a way better date than that kid Luis."

I felt my blush start. "It's not a *date*."

"Okay," Phoebe said in a such a weird voice I knew she was a) making fun of me and b) didn't believe me. "You said you needed help? Do you mean fixing that dress?"

I shook my head. "No, there's no help for that dress." As the words were leaving my mouth, I realized that my asking Calvin meant that he would *see* me in the Ruffle Monster.

"Hadn't thought of that part, huh?" Phoebe asked.

I shook my head. My best friend knew me too well. "Anyway, there's something else—another thing I hadn't thought of. My parents will be there, of course, and my cousins, and some other people who know I don't actually have a dog. But Calvin thinks that I do. Have a dog, I mean."

Phoebe gave me a look. "Ana, my friend. Just fess up about Osito already! It's not like you've been lying to him about the stash of nuclear weapons you hid in his garage!"

"That's a very weird—and oddly specific—scenario."

Phoebe waved a hand dismissively. "I've been doing this screenwriting thing online. That's not the point. The point is, this isn't, like, a terrible lie."

"Maybe not at first. But then I kept on telling it. And then I told lots of other lies that got all tangled up in the first one. It's a mess."

Phoebe patted my arm. "You already know what you have to do."

I let out a sigh. "Yeah. I know. I guess I just needed to hear somebody say it."

"I'll always be your somebody," Phoebe said. "Now come on, Charlotte. Let's figure out how you're going to break the truth to Calvin."

WEBSITE DESIGN IDEAS

IDEA #4:

Text alerts for liars.

Functions: Interactive database of lies and sub-lies flagged by key words.

Add: Voice recognition function—when liar says one of the key words, send an alert to phone. Maybe an electric shock.

Working-title ideas:

Liar Alert

Liar, Liar, Phone's on Fire

*Note: The functionality for this is not something you can actually create with your laptop. Maybe just start telling the truth???

14
Don't Leave Me

Phoebe helped me plan out what to say to Calvin, and I decided I'd talk to him at the park, away from school. I thought it might help if I had Osito with me, so Calvin could see, and remember, how much I loved that dog, even though he wasn't actually mine.

I nodded to myself, pleased with this idea, as I walked home from school. As soon as I turned the corner, though, I spotted an ambulance parked outside our building. I immediately felt a stab of fear. I raced inside and took the stairs two at a time. Halfway up the stairs to the fourth floor, I nearly collided with an EMT.

An EMT who was helping to carry Mrs. Ramirez on a stretcher. She was awake, I was relieved to see. She reached out a hand to place it on my arm, and the two men who were carrying her obeyed her plea for them to stop for a moment.

"Oh! Thank goodness, *mija*! I was hoping to find you!" Mrs. R said in a thin voice.

"Are you okay, Mrs. Ramirez?" I asked frantically. "What happened?"

Mrs. R shook her head weakly. "I had another fall. Listen, Ana. I called my daughter but she cannot come until Saturday. Please, *mija*, can you take Osito for me? Just until Saturday when my daughter gets here."

I stood staring at her in shock. My mother would never say yes . . . would she? The EMTs started moving again, and Mrs. R called out, "*Please* say that you will keep my Osito, Ana!"

And then I heard myself yelling after her, "Yes, Mrs. R. Don't worry! I'll take good care of him. I promise!"

I heard Mrs. R say, "Thank you, oh, thank you!" But I kept standing there frozen, my heart thumping so loud it seemed to echo in the empty stairwell.

What was I going to do? I'd just promised Mrs. R that I'd take Osito home with me for the rest of the week. There hadn't been anything else to do. The poor lady was being carried off to the hospital, and she was so worried about her dog. Of course I'd said yes.

And I had to try to convince my mom that we could keep Osito for a few days. Even in the middle of the quince craziness.

First, though, I needed to walk poor Osito, who was probably very upset and nervous upstairs after everything that had just happened with Mrs. R.

I shook myself and ran up to the fifth floor. I reached for my key, but the door was unlocked. When I walked in I called Osito's name, but he didn't come running like he usually did. My heart started pounding again—what if he'd run out the door in all the confusion with the paramedics? I started racing through the apartment, yelling, "Osito! Come here, boy! Osito! Where *are* you?"

I stopped yelling when I heard a small whimper. I followed the direction the sound had come from. I walked into Mrs. R's bedroom and heard the sound again. I knelt down on the worn brown carpet and peered under her bed. I couldn't see him in the dark, especially since he was all black, but I heard him again. I stretched out a hand and a few seconds later I felt a little wet tongue gently lick my hand.

"Come on out, boy," I cooed. Slowly, he wriggled out from under the bed. I picked him up and it made me sad to find that he was shaking very hard. I sat on the floor with my back against Mrs. R's nightstand and held Osito close against me, whispering that everything would be okay. After what seemed like a long time, my little bear finally stopped shaking.

I carried Osito out to the kitchen and put his supper in his bowl. He ate a few bites but then stopped, sat down on the floor, and stared up at me with his huge, round, black eyes. I felt like my heart was being squeezed tightly in a fist. Osito seemed like he was trying to tell me something.

I thought that it was probably "Don't leave me."

I took him outside so he could take care of his business. I didn't walk him all the way over to the park, since I knew I needed to tell Mom what had happened, and she was probably home from work by now.

I carried Osito upstairs and unlocked my door, trying to control my nerves. I *had* to ask Mom—I didn't have a choice. What else could I do with Osito until Mrs. R's daughter came on Saturday?

Mom turned around at the sound of the door and immediately spotted Osito.

"No, Ana, you know the rules. Take him back upstairs this minute. This apartment's barely big enough for the four of us, let alone an animal."

"But Mrs. Ramirez just had to go to the hospital this afternoon—in an ambulance! She begged me to look after Osito . . ."

Mom frowned. "What happened to Mrs. Ramirez? Is she all right?"

"Well, I don't know; she's going to the hospital, so I think probably she's been better."

Mom gave me a look. "Ana, let's try that again without the sarcasm?"

"I'm sorry." Ugh, what was wrong with me? I was supposed to be talking Mom into letting me keep Osito for a few days. Maybe I should have asked Tali for help. Tali knew how to bring out our mother's sweet side. Somehow, no matter how hard I tried, I always seemed to end up bringing out the other side. I took a deep breath.

"She said she fell again," I explained. "And she begged me to help her, Mom—what could I do?"

Mom's expression softened a bit. "I hear what you're saying, Ana, and I suppose I understand why you made such a hasty promise. But that doesn't change . . ." Mom was shaking her head, and I knew she was about to say no, in spite of everything.

I sat down heavily in a chair with Osito in my arms. Now what?

"Ana? Are you listening to me? I'm sure if you explain the situation to Dr. Medina he'll give you a break on the boarding fees. If you don't have enough from your allowance I can help you."

I stared at Mom, my mouth open. She was actually telling me to take Osito to the vet's office one block over and pay them to put him in a kennel until Mrs. R's daughter came to town.

"You understand why you need to help pay the kenneling fees, don't you, Ana?" Mom said. "You are the one who made the promise."

"Do you think I care about paying the money?" I stood up, still clutching Osito to my chest. "How can you even—I *just* told you what happened to his mom. I found him shaking under her bed. And you want me to just take him to a kennel!"

"Ana, calm down. You knew the rules before you made her that promise. I'm sorry about Mrs. Ramirez's fall, I really am, but that doesn't change anything about our house rules."

Now I was so mad *I* was shaking. I knew that Mom didn't feel the same way about Osito as I did. But I still didn't understand how she could be so cruel to him. Or to me.

"I'm not taking him to a kennel. I'll find someplace else—someplace where they actually care about animals—*and* people!"

I opened the door and walked out before she could say anything else. I slammed the door as best I could one-handed, since I was still carrying Osito. I walked quickly down the stairs, my heart thumping just as hard as it had on those same stairs a little while ago.

I walked all the way outside before I realized I didn't actually know where I was going. I knew for sure I wasn't going to take Osito to Dr. Medina's place. The thought of my poor little bear sitting alone all night in one of those little concrete stalls at his clinic made my heart hurt. Phoebe would always be my first call in a crisis, but I knew her dad was majorly allergic to dogs and cats.

And then I thought of a possible answer. I put Osito down beside me and started walking toward the park. I realized that the odds of Calvin being there now were pretty slim; it was later than the time we usually met. I pulled my phone out of my back pocket and started a text, but then I had no idea what to say. Besides, a text might not seem like an emergency, but if I called him . . .

I decided to go for it, hitting the call button before I had time to think any more about it.

After four rings, Calvin answered.

"Hey, Ana," he said, sounding only a little bit surprised that I was calling him.

"I'm so glad you answered!" I burst out. "Can you . . . could you meet me at the park? I have a situation and I really need . . . I'm hoping you can help me."

"I'll be right there," Calvin said.

I felt a surge of relief. I got to the dog run, let Osito off his leash, and watched him sniff around. I sat on a bench, holding my phone, trying to figure out what to say to Calvin when he got there.

I should just come clean and explain the WHOLE situation to him, was my first thought. But what if he got mad that I'd been lying to him—so mad that he refused to let Osito stay with him for the next four days? That idea seemed far from impossible.

The little bear was back from sniffing, and started pawing at my leg, wanting to be picked up. He'd had a hard day.

He was also looking up at me with the exact expression he'd been wearing before. His eyes were speaking to me clearly.

Don't leave me.

"Ana! Are you okay?" I looked up to see Calvin standing in

front of me, without Pancake. He sounded out of breath, like maybe he'd run here.

I met his eyes, and wanted so much to tell him the truth. But how could I risk it? When I looked down at Osito once more, I knew that I couldn't.

I took a deep breath and let it out, and then I started lying again.

15

Incomplete Fairy Tale

"I didn't know that Mom was having the apartment fumigated," I said to Calvin, while a small piece of my soul died. "I guess with all the quince madness she forgot to tell us."

I hated that I was lying. Again. But I'd decided to suck up feeling like dirt and do what was right for Osito.

Next I explained that we were staying with my uncle Victor, which was a ridiculous lie, since he lives in Philadelphia, but Calvin didn't know that. I said that I couldn't bring "my" dog with us because my cousin Mateo was allergic to all dogs. That part at least was true, not that it mattered. I didn't figure that one accidental truth in a giant sea of lies would win me any points at this stage of the game.

"Where do they live?" Calvin asked. "Your uncle's family."

I blinked at Calvin. "Oh, in the neighborhood." I waved a hand in the air. "I can walk there. So, what do you think?" I asked him, holding my breath. "Do you think your parents would say yes? If you don't mind asking, that is."

"I don't see why they wouldn't. And of course I'll ask them. I can see you're really upset about this."

I felt another sharp stab of guilt, this one in my heart. Calvin was so kind and thoughtful. And I was being basically awful. I looked down at Osito's little face to remind myself why.

"I know I could take him to a kennel or something. That's what my mom said to do. But I just . . . can't. He's never stayed in one of those places, and . . ."

"Say no more, I gotcha. So, hey—do you want to come to dinner at my house? That way you could get Osito settled and everything before you had to go back home."

I felt a smile spread across my face. That meant more time with Osito . . . and Calvin.

And more time before I had to go back and face Mom. I knew I'd be in trouble for walking out like that.

"I would love to!" I said. "If you're sure your parents won't mind . . ."

"They won't, I promise."

"Okay. Thanks, Calvin. I'll just text home to tell them."

He held out a hand and I realized he meant for me to give him Osito's leash and harness. I did, and then glanced down at my phone. I had a bunch of texts from Tali asking where I was and what had happened with Mom.

Calvin kept holding Osito's leash while I texted my sister back:

I'm ok will explain later. Tell Mom I'm finding a place 4 Osito and will be home later.

Tali immediately texted back:

What happened??? Mom seems mad but she wouldn't tell me.

Also where r u going??

I wrote back quickly:

To Calvin's 4 dinner but don't tell her that. Be home soon. XO A.

I turned off my phone then. I didn't want Tali—or worse, Mom—to keep calling and texting me. My only thought right now was to get Osito settled somewhere he felt safe.

When we got to Calvin's apartment, Calvin set Osito down on the floor and called out for Pancake. She came running fast—almost as fast as she'd been chasing that squirrel.

The two pugs shared their usual effusive greeting, though to me it seemed Osito still wasn't quite himself.

"Aw, it's like he knows you're going to have to leave him here," Calvin said quietly beside me.

"I know," I said, feeling miserable.

"It'll be okay!" Calvin said in a louder voice. "You can visit him every day."

What I couldn't say then was that this would be my last visit since I was probably going to be grounded until graduation.

High school graduation.

I followed Calvin into the kitchen. Mr. Palmer was doing the cooking this time. Calvin's mom was in DC on a business trip, and Chelsea was back at college.

"We're having white bean chili and homemade corn bread," Mr. Palmer said.

"Mmm, my favorite. Ana's going to join us," Calvin said.

"Cool," Mr. Palmer said. "I made a ton of chili."

"He always does," Calvin told me. "We end up eating it for, like, a week. It's good you're here to eat some of it—might give us one less chili day!"

Mr. Palmer chuckled. It seemed to me that the atmosphere at Calvin's house was a lot more relaxed than it usually was at mine. Plus, no one was having a quince in this family. I felt a twinge of jealousy.

"Hey, Dad?" Calvin added. "Is it okay if Ana's dog, Osito, stays with us for a few days? Her apartment's being fumigated."

I felt an enormous wave of guilt as Mr. Palmer nodded. "No problem," he said. "Pancake will be thrilled, of course. Does Osito need any special food or medicine?"

I shook my head, still guilt-stricken. "He can eat what

Pancake eats for now, but I'll bring over his food next time," I managed to say. Then I thanked Mr. Palmer and Calvin and I set the table for dinner.

Mr. Palmer brought out the pot of chili, the corn bread, and a container of butter, and Calvin came in with a pitcher of lemonade. We sat down and I took a bite of chili. Calvin was right; it was delicious. I felt a warm rustle of fur against my leg and peered down under the table to see Osito. As usual, Pancake was glued to his side.

What would happen now that Mrs. R was in the hospital? I'd found a place for Osito until Saturday. But what would happen when Mrs. R's daughter arrived?

I was afraid I already knew the answer to that. Mrs. R's daughter would probably take Osito, and Mrs. R when she was well enough, back to Baltimore with her.

"If you don't like the chili, Ana, I can make you something else," Mr. Palmer offered, his voice breaking into my thoughts.

"No!" I shook my head. "It's really yummy."

"You were just kind of stirring it, staring off into space," Calvin observed.

"I'm sorry. I had a fight with my mom, and it's just . . ."

"Say no more," Mr. Palmer said. "And I'm sure you'll make up with your mom when you go back home. Once everyone cools off after a fight, it's much easier to say you're sorry and move forward."

That was the problem, though. I wasn't sorry I'd left, or found another option for Osito.

And I also knew that Mom wasn't sorry for her part, either. So where did that leave us?

After dinner, I hugged Osito tightly and kissed his furry head, then told Calvin I didn't need him to walk me home. It was still light enough outside to go alone. Plus, I was pretty sure I was about to cry, and I didn't want Calvin to see.

When I got home, I stood at the door to our apartment, hand hovering over the doorknob, afraid to go inside. This was new territory. I'd never *really* gotten in trouble. Sure, Mom and I argued pretty often, but it was always over little stuff. I'd certainly never run out of the house like that, and stayed away for three hours. I didn't know what to expect, but I knew for a fact that it wasn't going to be good.

Okay, Ana, time to quit stalling and face your consequences. I took what was quite possibly my last gulp of free air, turned the doorknob, and walked inside.

The apartment was strangely quiet. I looked around, then jumped a little when I saw Mom sitting at her place at the kitchen table, waiting for me.

"Hi," I said in a tiny voice.

"Is that all you've got to say?" Mom asked.

I shook my head. "I was waiting. For the yelling to start."

Mom frowned and opened her mouth, but then she closed it. She exhaled and waited a few more seconds before speaking again.

"I'm not going to yell. Your father and I had a talk."

Had Papi taken my side?

"You know he had that dog growing up. Boneyard or something."

Mom didn't say anything else right away, so I provided the dog's actual name. "Barnard."

"Yes, I guess that was it. You know I don't really get the

whole pet thing. I never had one. But your father explained to me that your . . . attachment to this dog, even though he's not actually yours, would have made it very hard for you to say no to Mrs. Ramirez. Or to take him to the kennel, as I suggested. So . . . I'm trying to understand how you feel about that animal, is what I'm trying to say. But I have to say I'm still surprised you would have said yes to Mrs. Ramirez. You didn't honestly think that I'd agree that you could keep him here?"

I swallowed hard. "I was just worried about Osito, and Mrs. R. If I'd been thinking clearly I would have known not to say yes. I know that once you decide something you're not ever going to change your mind no matter what."

Mom drew her breath in sharply as if something I'd said surprised her, though I couldn't think what it would have been. After all, we were in the middle of talking about how she never changed.

After a few more seconds, Mom continued talking, though her voice sounded weird. I wondered if she was still really mad at me, but keeping it under control because she'd promised Papi.

"I'm going to give you tonight's temper tantrum as your one free pass. And I do mean *one*—as in, this is the only one you'll ever get. Got it?"

I nodded quickly. "Got it."

"And no matter what, you should not have run out like that. That's not okay."

"I know. I texted Tali . . ."

"She told us where you were. Go do your homework now. We won't talk about this again."

"Okay," I said, rising. I felt relieved, but not as relieved as I would have expected to feel. Mom seemed really—well, she seemed sad, but that didn't make sense. She couldn't have been too worried about me, since Tali had told them where I was.

I turned back around. "Good night," I told Mom.

She was just sitting in her chair, fiddling with the handle of her tea mug. She looked up and said, "Good night, Ana."

Tali had clearly been listening at the door to our room, since I almost tripped over her as soon as I opened the door. She enfolded me in a big hug. "I'm so glad you're home!"

"Me, too. I'm mostly glad I survived the talk with Mom."

"I didn't hear any yelling?" Tali sounded as confused as I felt.

"She didn't yell. She said Papi talked to her."

"He did, but I couldn't hear what they said."

"Not for lack of trying, I'm sure." I gave her a pointed look.

Tali gave me a sheepish look back. "I was worried about you!"

"Nice job telling them exactly where I was, by the way."

"Ana! Papi said they were going to call the police unless I told them—I didn't have a choice."

"You fell for that?"

"I think he was serious, Ana."

"I guess I'm just lucky he didn't go over there and embarrass me."

"I know, I was kind of afraid of that, too," Tali said with another sheepish smile. "But tell me how it went with Calvin's parents."

I sat down heavily on the edge of my bed and started to unlace my boots. "It was just his dad. It was fine."

"Oh, okay. So, let me get this straight. Mom didn't yell, and you're not crying, so she must not have grounded you for the rest of your life?"

"She didn't even punish me," I said.

"She didn't give you a consequence at all?"

"Not yet," I said. I had a sudden, terrible thought: What if the whole free-pass thing had meant a free pass just for *tonight*?

"That's kind of weird, actually. Mom's always hardest on you."

I looked up at Tali in surprise. "She is?"

"Of course she is. You never noticed?"

"I guess not. I mean, you almost never do anything wrong."

Tali stuck her tongue out at me. "I can't help being naturally good. But I think it's because you're so smart. Like she was."

"What do you mean? She's still smart."

"Well, of course she is, but she didn't get to really *do* anything with her smarts, is what I mean. I think she regrets it, at least sometimes—not finishing college. I think she's so hard on you because she wants to be sure that you do. That you get to use your giant brain for something amazing."

"You're smart, too!" I pointed out.

"I know, but not like you."

I shook my head. "I'm just obsessed with studying, is all . . ."

Tali shook her head. "Don't be so humble, Ana. You're first in your class."

Maybe, I thought.

"But *you're* the sweet one," I said.

"Not everything's so black and white, *hermanita*. You're not the only one who's smart, and I'm not the only one who's sweet. We're both a mixture—with lots of different parts to our personalities."

I looked at my sister for a few moments. "You're right. See, you're not only smart, you're *wise*."

"It's because I'm *almost* an official woman," Tali said with a wink. "The countdown has begun."

I looked at the calendar over my desk and realized she was right. In a week and a half, I'd be wearing that crazy dress and dancing at Tali's party . . . with Calvin.

In the meantime I just hoped that Mom really wasn't going to ground me. There was no way I could ever explain *not* visiting Osito to Calvin.

And as much as I hated the thought of not seeing Osito, the thought of Calvin thinking badly of me was almost worse. He'd been so amazing, running all the way to the park when I called him, taking in "my" dog. Like a real-life Prince Charming.

My eyes traveled to the Ruffle Monster still hanging on the back of my closet door.

So much for my life as a complete fairy tale, I thought. In those stories, some fairy godmother always saved the heroine from having to wear the hideously awful dress.

But at least, thanks to Calvin, I didn't have to go to the quince alone. And Osito wasn't in doggy jail. It had been a long, bad day, but if it weren't for Calvin, it could have been a lot worse.

16

It's a Sister Thing

"Are you baking?" Mom asked when she came home from work the next day.

"Yep. I felt like it," I said, stirring cookie dough in the bowl.

That was a lie, too, though a pretty little one, all things considered. I wanted to have something to bring over to the Palmers' tonight; I thought maybe I'd feel less guilty about everything if I didn't show up empty-handed.

"This is Abuelita Elena's recipe," I explained. I was making two batches of snickerdoodles—one for my family as well. A small, sugary peace offering.

"That's great," Mom said, but she sounded distracted. She hadn't even changed out of her work clothes and already she was banging the cabinet doors open and closed, getting out things to start dinner. I wondered if I was in her way with my cookie making.

"I promised your father I'd make *pastelillos* tonight," Mom said in a tired voice. "He got his promotion at work today."

"That's great!" I exclaimed. I knew Papi had been working toward that for a long time. I also knew that *pastelillos*, while delicious—my stomach growled just thinking of the ground beef and potatoes cased inside fried dough—were a lot of work. And Mom already sounded tired.

"Hey, why don't you go and change and I'll get everything out for you for the *pastelillos*?" I offered. "And the cookies are ready to go in the oven so I'll clean all this up fast, too. I didn't mean to get in your way."

Mom closed a cabinet door—more quietly this time—and turned to face me. "You didn't know about the promotion. And the cookies will be a nice addition to our little celebration. But I will take you up on the offer to help. Thank you. I'll just get the recipe out . . ."

"I don't need to see the recipe!" I told her. "I've had it memorized for years."

Mom smiled at me, patted my arm, and went back to her room to change. I hurried to put the cookies in the oven, and then got out everything for the *pastelillo* dough. Then I got out two big onions and started chopping them very fine. Mom would want to make the dough herself, but I didn't think she'd have a problem with my doing the boring chopping part.

"Oh, you already chopped the onions!" she exclaimed when she came back out wearing a T-shirt and jeans, looking younger than she had in her work clothes. "Wonderful!"

"I thought you wouldn't mind."

"Mind! Ah, *mija*, I'm thrilled! It's been a long day at work. I'll take all the help I can get."

The timer dinged for my cookies, and I pulled them out of the oven. They looked perfect.

"I do have to go visit Osito in a few minutes," I told her. "I promised I'd bring his food over." I added the last part in a burst of inspiration, so Mom would know that I really had to go.

"Okay, I understand. How is Mrs. Ramirez doing?"

A hot wave of embarrassment crashed over my head as I realized that I didn't know. "I'm going to check on her at the hospital after I drop off the food."

"I don't want you going there alone, Ana. I don't mind you going to the Palmers' since it's in the neighborhood. I'll go with you to check on Mrs. Ramirez, if you want, but it will have to wait until tomorrow."

"I understand. I bet I can find her daughter's number upstairs and maybe get an update that way today." I started packing up some of the cookies I'd made to take to Calvin.

"That's a good idea, but only if she has it lying out some-where. Don't go snooping through all her things."

I raised one hand. "No snooping. Scout's honor. Okay, I've got all the spices out for you. I'm going to run upstairs now, then over to the Palmers', and be back for dinner."

"All right, Ana. Text me when you get there. Okay?"

"Will do."

I raced upstairs and grabbed a bag of Osito's food. Then I found a Post-it on the fridge with the number for Mrs. Ramirez's daughter, Rosa. *See, Mom—I didn't snoop.*

I raced back down the stairs, taking them two at a time, then fast-walked over to the park.

I breathed a sigh of relief when I saw that Calvin was still there with both dogs.

Osito and Pancake looked like best friends—they seemed to be playing doggy hide-and-seek around the legs of the bench Calvin was sitting on.

"Hey! Look who it is, Osito!" Calvin called.

Osito came barreling toward me. I knelt down to hug him, but he was wriggling too much.

"I brought some of his food from . . . home," I said, gesturing to the bag.

"You didn't need to—he seems perfectly okay with what Pancake eats. But I'll take it back. Besides, you were pretty rattled yesterday. I still can't believe your mom set up that fumigation without giving you a heads-up—since he can't stay at your uncle's."

"My mom's not really all that dog-oriented."

"Surprising that she let you have a pet, then."

"Yep, it's kind of a miracle. Oh, hey, I brought you some cookies I made, too."

We both laughed as Pancake came running over to us at the word *cookies*.

Calvin laughed. "Sorry, girl, these are for me. Hey, did you bake these?" he asked me.

I nodded. "Fresh out of the oven."

A grin spread over Calvin's face. "That's so sweet of you, Ana."

He seemed so happy that somehow it made me feel worse. Here Calvin was, thinking I was sweet. He had no idea how wrong he was.

The second Mrs. R's daughter came to claim Osito, I would come clean about everything.

I was distracted from this stressful thought by Osito pawing at my leg, whining for me to pick him up.

I remembered that the relief I'd feel after fessing up to Calvin was going to be served with a heaping dose of sadness. I had to assume Mrs. R's daughter would be taking O back with her to Maryland. I might never see him again.

I scooped him up and cuddled him close while I had him with me.

"You okay?" Calvin asked.

I nodded and said yes.

And even that was a lie.

The next day at lunch I slid a foil-wrapped packet across the table with a wink. Phoebe squealed in delight.

"Is this what I think it is?"

I nodded. "Two of Mama Ramos's famous *pastelillos*. I had to put them in my room during dinner or somebody would have eaten them for sure."

Phoebe paused in opening the foil. "These were in your room all night?"

"I said during *dinner*." I threw a napkin across the table at her. "I wouldn't go to all the trouble of saving them if I was just going to let them spoil overnight, silly."

"Oh, okay, thank goodness. Because I was all excited for *pastelillos*. That would have been heartbreaking."

"So how's your coding project coming?" I asked as Phoebe tore into my mom's delicacy. "Do you still want me to help you on Sunday?"

"Soundsgoodwecanworkatmyhouse."

"Maybe tell me *after* you finish eating."

She swallowed. "I was just saying sure—we can work at my house if you want."

"Oh! Good. How far have you gotten with your site coding?"

"Um, I've thought about what I want it to do."

"Phoebe!"

"I perform best under pressure."

"But if you don't start until the last minute you can't really go above and beyond with your project. If you start early . . ."

"I'm fine with doing the standard project."

"Must be nice," I grumbled.

"Procrastinating? It's okay, I guess."

"No, I meant, not feeling the need to do anything extra. What's that like?"

"It's very relaxing," Phoebe told me. "Too bad you'll never experience it."

I felt weird being dogless in the dog run, but I knew Calvin would be there soon with Osito and Pancake. I turned excitedly when I heard the gate open, but it was a lady with a standard poodle. She looked a little bit like the queen from *The Princess Diaries*, so she had the perfect dog.

But the very next creak of the gate was him. I stood up and waved, and sat down so that Osito could run into my lap. I looked up at Calvin.

"Thanks for bringing him. I know it's probably harder to walk two dogs."

He sat down beside me. "I think I'm up to that challenge. Speaking of challenges, I was hoping to run my coding project past you. Maybe tomorrow? I have time in the afternoon."

Tomorrow. The day Mrs. R's daughter was coming. The day I would tell Calvin the truth.

"I'm not sure about Saturday, but I'll totally help you. Maybe on Sunday?"

"Sunday works. I've also got this huge project for language arts class due right after the coding one. But my partner's been really good. She's done a lot of the research already."

"Oh, who is it?"

"Lucy Alvarez."

I heard Phoebe's voice in my head, telling me about how on Calvin's first day, Lucy had said he was cute. Was Lucy being so helpful because she liked Calvin? What if he liked her back?

Ugh! Like I didn't have too much to think about already, here I was wondering about Lucy Alvarez's romantic life.

Except *that* wasn't what I was really wondering.

I was thinking that I didn't want Calvin to fall for some other girl before I could tell him the truth. Or how after tomorrow, Calvin might be mad at me, and Lucy would be there waiting . . .

That thought made it hard to breathe. I stood up. "I can't stay. I have to go to the hospital," I said.

"What? Are you okay?"

"No—I mean, yes, I'm okay. But I have to visit my neighbor.

She fell and got hurt. And she's all alone in there until her daughter comes to the city tomorrow."

"That's really nice of you. Do you want me to go with you? I could take the dogs back first . . ."

"No, that's okay. My mom's going with me. We're going to bring her some soup." *And the news that her dog is doing just fine.* I gave Osito one more hug.

"So your place will be ready to go back to tomorrow, huh?" Calvin asked.

I nodded. "I'll come over in the morning to pick up Osito?"

"Sure," Calvin said. "See you tomorrow."

When I got home, Mom had left me a note saying that she had to stay late at work but Tali could go with me to the hospital to see Mrs. R, as long as we kept in touch by text.

Tali came out of our room. She picked up a small white bag that was sitting on the counter. "Mom asked me to get the soup—I got Italian wedding. Hope Mrs. R likes it."

"Thanks for getting it. I was just . . ."

"Hanging out with your boyfriend."

My face flamed. "He's not my—he's doing a project with Lucy Alvarez in his language arts class," I added, then slapped my palm over my mouth. "Ugh, why do I always tell you too much?"

"'Cause, whatever it is, you *want* to talk about it, and you know you can say anything to me." Tali linked her arm through mine as we walked. "It's a sister thing. So tell me more about this Lucy Alvarez . . ."

Mrs. Ramirez was sleeping when we got to her room at the hospital. One of her nurses woke her up.

"She's been lonely for visitors," the nurse explained to me and Tali. "She'd never forgive me if I told her she slept through some."

"Hi, Mrs. R," I said as she blinked awake and smiled at me.

"We got you some soup," Tali said, and handed her the bag.

"Oh, from the deli! Bless you, girls! But how is my Osito, Ana? Is he doing all right at your place?"

I exchanged a look with Tali. I hoped she could handle this one for me. I couldn't bear another lie.

Thankfully, Tali picked up my brain waves and said, "Osito's doing great, very happy, though of course he misses you."

"Rosa will be here tomorrow," Mrs. R said. "She'll take Osito home with her until I'm back on my feet."

I planned to get Osito from Calvin's in the morning, and then I could hang out at Mrs. R's apartment until her daughter came. Hopefully, I could finally make some real progress on my coding project while I waited.

Tali and I stayed for a few more minutes, and Mrs. R thanked us about eight more times for the soup. I realized that I definitely should have come to visit her before today.

On the way downstairs in the elevator, I said to Tali, "Wow, that was amazing—you didn't actually *lie* to Mrs. R, but you made her feel better about Osito. I knew you'd know the right thing to say."

Tali gave me a strange look. "It was still lying, Ana. You know that, right? But in this case, Mrs. R doesn't know Calvin or his family, so telling her would only have upset her. Meanwhile, you do know them, and Osito's being well taken care of. So in my view it wouldn't have actually been kind to tell her the truth."

"I hope I did the right thing."

"You did what you thought was best. That's all anybody can do."

"Ugh, there you go being wise again."

"With age comes great wisdom," Tali said in a low voice. We both laughed as we stepped out onto the sidewalk. It's not like the joke was all that funny, really, but Tali was right. It was a sister thing.

That night after dinner I took the dishes over to the sink and started to rinse them.

"What are you doing?" Mom asked.

"The dishes."

She narrowed her eyes at me. "What are you after?"

I felt hurt that my doing something nice made Mom suspicious. "You had to work late, then cook. Papi just got home, and Tali did me a favor by going to the hospital with me and getting the soup. So dishes are me tonight."

Mom didn't say anything else, but I thought I saw her give Papi a look.

I kept washing dishes. While I worked, I thought of ways I could improve my Waggle Walkers site. The ideas were swirling around in my head as I finished the last dish, stacked it in the overflowing drying rack, and went back to my room to work on the coding.

Tali was sitting at her desk, staring at her computer screen. "Did you finish your paper?" I asked her.

"No. I still need another two hundred words, but I have no idea what else to write. What else can you say about talking pigs?"

"Oh, your paper is on *Animal Farm*?"

She spun around to face me. "It annoys me that you know that based on the phrase *talking pigs*."

I laughed. "I challenge you to think of another important work of literature that phrase would apply to! Besides *Charlotte's Web*, of course."

Tali didn't laugh at that, she just frowned harder. "I guess you've read it, then. For fun or something."

"Well, not fun exactly—when we were learning about the Russian Revolution in history last year, Mrs. Albaño mentioned the book, so I took it out of the library," I explained. "I wasn't sure I was gonna read the whole thing, but then it was so short, I did."

"Ugh, I'd be annoyed at your overachieving, but it means now you can help me."

Tali got up and pointed at the computer, so I sat down and started reading.

"Tali, this is really good," I said after reading the first few paragraphs. "You make a great point about Snowball the pig." I looked up at her. "Why are you being so hard on yourself?"

Her eyes goggled out at me. "Wait, did I miss the announcement about backward day? Did *you* just tell *me* to stop being hard on myself?"

"What do you mean?" I asked.

"*Nobody* is harder on themselves than you, Ana. Don't you remember your science fair meltdown in fifth grade?"

"That doesn't count."

"Oh, please. You totally freaked because you didn't think your project was good enough. And it won third place."

"Yes, and everybody knows third place feels just like first."

"See what I mean! Besides, sis—I've never won third place at anything."

"Um, are you forgetting every first-place medal in the world at dance?" I pointed to the bookshelf where she kept her trophies and medals.

"I meant school stuff, Ana."

"Oh, well, then—sorry. I wasn't trying to be bratty about the whole third-place thing," I said softly. "I've never won a medal for anything *except* school stuff. But that science fair freak-out was a one-time thing. I'm not usually like that . . ."

"*Hermanita*, I know you better than anybody. School's your thing. You take it very seriously, and that's okay. But just remember, you can't control everything."

I was about to argue with her, but then I realized she was right. It wasn't a great feeling, though.

17

Order of Operations

Sometime around midnight, Tali threw one of her stuffed animals at my head.

"Hey!"

"You're thrashing around so much over there now I can't sleep!"

I sat up, finding Mr. Stuffins the penguin and throwing him back over to her. "I'm nervous about telling Calvin the truth."

"I'm sure Calvin will forgive you, once you explain."

"Are you sure?" I whispered across our dark room.

"Well, I don't see how I can be one hundred percent sure. But if he's really your friend, I think he will."

"I hope so."

"Okay. Now go to sleep."

I lay there for a few more minutes, feeling completely and totally awake. I hated when things were undecided. I decided to give up on sleep for the time being.

"I can't sleep," I told my sister. "I'm going to go to the bathroom and do some coding."

"Oh, Ana—this is not normal behavior."

"I'm willing to concede that point," I said as I gathered up the laptop and a pillow to sit on and headed to the bathroom.

The next morning, exhausted from lack of sleep, I walked over to Calvin's apartment to pick up Osito. Tali had agreed to come with me for moral support, since this was supposed to be the moment when I spilled the beans to Calvin. But when we arrived at the Palmers' place, Calvin wasn't there. Mrs. Palmer told us that he'd gone out earlier that morning to play hockey with his dad.

"I'll bet you're glad to have your dog back," Mrs. Palmer said as Osito leaped into my arms. I felt a stab of sadness somewhere near my heart, since I was just about to say good-bye to him— possibly forever.

I thanked Mrs. Palmer, patted Pancake, and left with Tali.

When the elevator doors closed, I turned to my sister. "Calvin wasn't there! Now when am I going to tell him?" I cried.

"You can call him tonight. Or meet him in the park tomorrow."

I looked down at Osito. "I can't imagine going there without Osito," I said. "I can't believe he's probably moving to Maryland today!"

"It's just until Mrs. Ramirez gets better, Ana. Don't borrow trouble."

I shook my head. "Mrs. R hasn't been doing so well. Even before her last fall, it was taking her about twenty minutes to make it up the stairs. I'm not sure how much longer she can go on living on the fifth floor in a building with no elevator—even without Osito take care of. Her daughter may want Mrs. R to come live with her, too."

"That's so sad. I didn't know things had gotten so bad for Mrs. R." Tali had tears in her eyes.

"Oh, Tali—I didn't mean to make you cry. I just meant it wasn't only Osito I was worried about."

Tali and I got back to our building and climbed the steps to the fifth floor. I used the key and let us in and took Osito off his leash so he could run across the living room. I hit the switch for the overhead light, since Mrs. Ramirez had left her curtains pulled shut.

"Ana, is it always like this?" Tali asked.

I looked around. When I'd been there last, I'd been so panicked looking for Osito that I hadn't noticed, but the apartment was really a mess. There were several empty Styrofoam containers from the deli, and a bunch of empty Canada Dry cans. Mrs. R seemed to have been eating in the living room and not really cleaning up after herself.

It was worse in the kitchen. The sink was full of dirty dishes, as was the countertop. I saw a roach scurry across the counter so I picked up my shoe and whacked it.

"It's *not* usually like this," I said in answer to Tali's question.

"She must not have been feeling well enough to look after things."

"We need to clean up in here," I said. I gave my backpack one last look—I'd brought along my computer and notebooks to work on my project. But I knew I couldn't leave Mrs. R's place like this, whether she ended up coming back to it or not.

"Are you sure? I know you have a lot of work to do for your coding project," Tali said. "I could clean . . ."

"I'm not going to just sit there while I let you deal with this," I told her, shaking my head resolutely. "Besides, this isn't a one-person job. It's not even a two-person one," I added, pulling out my phone. "I'll text Phoebe."

"Maybe Mrs. R's daughter should see this, though, Ana?" Tali said. "I mean, she needs to know what's been going on."

"Mrs. R says her daughter works two jobs, and she has three little kids. *And* Mrs. R told me that one of them has special needs and takes a lot of Rosa's attention. How about if we take a couple of pictures, and if it seems like we need to convince Rosa that her mom needs more help, we can show them to her. But for now let's try to fix this." I waved a hand around to indicate the terrible mess in the kitchen.

"Okay, where do we start?"

I knelt down on the sticky floor and opened the cabinet below the sink to check for cleaning supplies. I rattled a bottle of cleaning spray. "There's a half bottle of this, and it's got bleach in it. But I don't see anything for the floor. Maybe run downstairs and grab our Swiffer and some wet pads?" I told Tali.

"On it." Tali nodded, and was gone.

I looked over at Osito. "I'm sorry I let you guys down," I told him. "I was too busy wrapped in my own stupid stuff."

I felt beyond foolish to have been so worried about the accidental lie I'd told to Calvin about Osito. While I'd been worrying about myself . . . my feelings, Mrs. R had really been struggling. And I hadn't even noticed.

I stood up and started in on the dishes in the sink. I had to fill some of the cups and bowls with water and soap so they could soak. The rest I washed and dried and started to put away.

I heard a knock at the door, walked over, and opened it to

find Phoebe, holding a bucket. "My mom said we might need supplies," she told me, and I gave her a big hug.

"Wow, I guess you really did need those supplies," she said. "Are you okay?"

"I've been an idiot," I told her. "But I'll work on fixing that later. For now, thank you for helping me!"

I showed her around some of the problems we'd already found. "The bathroom needs some TLC, too," Phoebe observed.

"I'll take that," I said. "We all share that duty at home, so no biggie."

Tali came back just then with our Swiffer and some gloves. I put on a pair, and used the scrubbing cleanser that Phoebe had brought to start in on the bathroom.

Phoebe took over for me in the kitchen, and Tali walked around with a trash bag picking up containers and cans. Then she started dusting in the living room. When I finished the bathroom, I decided that we should do Mrs. R's laundry, too, since she probably hadn't done that in a while. I pulled the sheets off her bed, grabbed some towels that had been out in the bathroom, and opened the door to head down to the laundry room.

I heard a shriek as a little girl standing in the hallway spotted me. I realized it was one of Mrs. Ramirez's grandchildren. Rosa was standing behind her.

"Oh, Ana, right?" Rosa said. "Hi—what's up with the laundry?"

I stood aside so that Rosa and the kids—two girls and a boy—could walk in.

"We were just cleaning up a little bit," I explained. "We didn't want to leave it like it was . . ."

Rosa's eyes filled with tears and she gave a sad smile. "I was worried how my mom was getting on. But every time I'd call she'd just tell me she was fine, and I have so much at home . . ." She started crying, and so I put down the laundry basket and gave her a hug.

"You live far away," I told her. "How could you have known? I'm just sorry I wasn't helping more. But I promise I will from now on. I mean, if she needs it." *If she still lives here.*

"You *have* been helping her, Ana! You're the one who walks Osito!"

At the sound of his name, Osito came trotting over. He wagged his tail and sniffed Rosa's sneakers, then hurried over to sniff the little kids' shoes. They giggled.

"The Osito part was selfish," I admitted. "I really love that dog."

"Well, you still helped her. And here you all are on a Saturday, cleaning, when I'm sure you have better things to do."

Tali and Phoebe had heard us talking and come out to the living room, both still wearing gloves and holding sponges.

"This is my sister, Tali, and my best friend, Phoebe," I said.

"Thank you both so much for helping out my mother this way," Rosa said.

"I'm glad we could help," Tali said. "Did you get to the hospital? How is Mrs. Ramirez doing?"

"We just came from there," Rosa said, nodding. "She's being released tomorrow, but I don't think she can stay here with those stairs."

I nodded, my stomach sinking, and I glanced down at Osito, who was playing with one of his chew toys.

Just then, Rosa's son, who didn't seem to speak, sat down on the floor and made a sound of distress. Rosa went over to calm him down. I looked at the two little girls and waved. They smiled shyly back at me.

Rosa straightened up and looked over at me. "Hey, Ana, I don't suppose you'd be willing to keep Osito a while longer, would you?"

My face fell. This was exactly what I wanted, except I couldn't say yes.

"Actually, my parents said I couldn't keep him in our apartment," I explained. "So he's been staying with one of my friends from school. I've seen him every day . . . but I didn't tell your mom. I didn't want to worry her . . ."

Rosa waved a hand. "Of course not, I'm glad you didn't tell her. And don't worry about keeping him longer—I shouldn't have asked. It's all just a little overwhelming right now with everything going on with Mom. Listen, we're staying with a friend of mine tonight, and heading back home tomorrow. I'm planning to bring Mom back to Maryland with me. But let me just take the kids over to my friend's place and I'll come right back and help you get this place straightened out."

"No, Rosa—we can get everything done here."

"Yes, we're nearly done," Tali told her.

"Are you sure?"

"Totally," I said. "I've got all of Osito's things together—I'll just get them for you." I swallowed past the lump in my throat as I realized that the moment was actually here. I was about to say good-bye to Osito.

Oh, if only Mom would reconsider. He could stay with us until Mrs. Ramirez got back on her feet. But Mom had made it very clear this past week that would never happen.

"Can I just take a second and say good-bye to him?" I asked Rosa, and she nodded.

I sat down on the floor and pulled Osito into my lap. "Hey, little guy. You're going to go on a trip. And I might not see you. But I sure will miss you. You be a good boy, okay?" I was crying now, because he was giving me those *don't leave me* eyes again.

But there was nothing I could do. I dried my tears, picked him up, and handed him to Rosa.

"Thank you again for everything, Ana."

"It was nothing," I whispered.

When they were gone, I sat down on Mrs. R's sofa, and Phoebe and Tali sat down, one on either side of me.

"I'm sorry, sis," Tali said. "I know how much you love Osito."

"I can't believe how rigid your mom is being," Phoebe added. "It would have been better for everybody if he could have just stayed with you."

"Not helping, Phoebe," Tali told her in a stern voice.

"Sorry! I call it like I see it."

"We know," Tali and I said in unison.

"I just hate seeing you upset, A," Phoebe said.

"I deserve it. I've messed everything up. I haven't been following the order of operations."

"You mean like in math? How you do the thing with the parentheses first?" Phoebe asked.

"No—I mean, yes—but I meant the order of operations

of, like, life. Mrs. R needed a lot more help than I was giving her."

"You didn't know," Tali said soothingly. "Now that you do, you are helping her."

"I should have paid better attention. But I'm going to, from now on." I stood up. "Okay, what's left to do?"

I took the laundry downstairs, and Phoebe and Tali took out the garbage. Finally, the place was as clean as we could make it.

I turned off the lights and was the last one out so I could lock the door. I spotted one of Osito's toys that I'd missed when I packed up his stuff, and I said a silent prayer that he would be happy in Maryland.

And then, I couldn't help it, I added a selfish thought—that I might see him again soon.

18

Worse Than Lying

"Hey, it's Calvin! Leave a message if you want."

I panicked and hit the button to hang up. It was Sunday morning. I'd waited until after we got home from church to try calling Calvin.

Usually, I would send a text message, but Calvin wasn't always the fastest at texting back. But the one time I'd called him, he'd answered right away.

I decided to call back and leave a voice mail—but I also decided that I should plan out what to say. I opened up one of my spiral notebooks and wrote it out:

Hi, Calvin, it's Ana. I'm sorry to bother you on Sunday.

I was sort of really hoping to talk to you today if you have time.

Call me back if you get this, and maybe we could meet at the park?

I took a deep breath, called again, and read the message I'd written down. He might wonder what was wrong with me, since I sounded a lot like a robot when I said it, but at least I'd gotten it all out.

I hoped he'd call back soon. But he didn't. And since his phone would show that I'd already called *twice*, I couldn't bring myself to dial his number a third time.

The day passed slowly. I caught up on all my homework, and worked a little on my coding project, but I kept getting distracted. First I got up to go get a snack, but Mom chased me out of the kitchen since she was making a huge Sunday dinner. So I walked downstairs, figuring I needed some fresh air. Then I found myself walking all the way to the park. Because, what if

Calvin was actually at the park right now, and I was torturing myself waiting for him to call? Maybe he'd dropped his phone in a toilet or something and that's why he hadn't gotten my message.

When I got to the dog run, it was full of people, but Calvin wasn't one of them. I sat down on one of the benches, just looking around at all the happy dog owners. Today, Osito was going to Baltimore with Rosa.

It was like there was a ball of ice in my stomach. I was worried about Osito, and Mrs. R. And I dreaded telling Calvin how I'd been lying to him.

I finally found Calvin on Monday morning at his locker.

"I called you yesterday," I said, walking over to him. "Oh, and also hi."

"Also hi to you, too. I'm sorry I didn't get your message until late. We all went sailing yesterday. Mom never lets us bring our phones, since one time Chelsea dropped hers in the river."

"Oh, that makes sense," I said. I guessed my premonition about a phone in water hadn't been completely off the mark.

"So what's up?" Calvin asked.

Here it was. The time had finally come.

"I have something to tell you," I said, my throat dry. "It's actually kind of funny how it all got started, really—it was just a misunderstanding, and I should've corrected you, but then I didn't, for some reason, and then it felt like it was too late to say anything . . ."

"Ana? I was hoping to check in with Mr. Bowen before the bell—we've got a test, you know."

"Yes. Okay." I took a deep breath and let it out. "Osito's not my dog."

Calvin's forehead wrinkled in confusion. "What? What are you talking about? Do you mean *Osito* is like a nickname or something?"

I shook my head. "No, that's his actual name. But the thing is . . . he doesn't actually belong to me."

Calvin looked even more confused. "I don't get what you're trying to say."

I said the rest fast to get it over with. My heart was racing and my words started coming out just as quickly. "Osito is my neighbor Mrs. Ramirez's dog. I would always walk him for her, since she has trouble going up and down the stairs in our building. That's why I would bring him to the dog run. But he wasn't . . . mine."

Calvin blinked, looking as if he was slowly starting to understand.

"Osito isn't—he was never yours?" Calvin repeated.

"That's right." I swallowed.

"Okay, so . . . basically you're saying that not only have you been lying to me for all this time, you also tricked me into keeping your *neighbor's* dog . . . for some reason."

"It's not like that!" My heart had skipped at least three beats at his words—and his tone of voice. "I mean, Osito does belong to Mrs. R, but I came home from school and she was being taken to the hospital in an ambulance, and she asked me to promise to look out for him so I did and I guess I thought that my mom would say it was okay for him to just stay at our place for a couple of nights, but then, she didn't . . ." Finally I had to take a breath.

Calvin put up a hand. His lips were drawn. "Ana, you still lied to me, though—right?"

"I did, but I was just so worried about Osito and I couldn't imagine sending him to a kennel when he was so upset and . . ."

"I get that you care about Osito. But I just really don't understand why you wouldn't have told me the truth. Even if you didn't think it was important enough to say something before, I don't get why you wouldn't say anything when you were asking me if he could stay at my house. You told me your place was being fumigated. I guess you made that up. But I don't see why you would have done that."

"I was afraid that . . ."

Something in Calvin's face changed. He'd figured out what I'd been about to say. "You were afraid I wouldn't let Osito stay if you told me the truth." Calvin slammed his locker door shut. He didn't meet my eyes. "Wow, you really have a high opinion of me."

"No—I mean, I do have a high opinion of you. A *super* high opinion! But Osito was just so upset, when I found him under . . ."

"I have to go, Ana."

He walked away without saying anything else.

I stood frozen. As many times as I'd imagined telling Calvin the truth, I had never imagined it going *that* badly. Of course I'd been worried he'd be mad—it was why I'd waited.

Worse than lying, it turned out, was the fact that I hadn't trusted Calvin to help Osito no matter what.

I trudged toward my own locker on feet that felt like lead. I'd been hoping for relief, but instead, I felt ten times more terrible than I had five minutes ago.

WEBSITE DESIGN IDEAS

IDEA #5:

Time machine.

I would like to invent a time machine so that I can go back in time and NOT lie to Calvin or mess everything up so badly. ☹

Functions: Nothing major, just figure out how to bend the space-time continuum.

19

For the Best

I hadn't heard from Mrs. R's daughter, so on Tuesday, I sent her a text, asking after her mother and Osito. She said they had both come with her to Baltimore and that her mother was recovering well. Rosa also thanked me again for cleaning up the apartment. It had been a huge help, she said, because the landlord was listing the place to rent, and now he could show it to people without it needing to be cleaned.

I figured that was probably it. I'd likely never see Mrs. R or Osito again.

It took me until Tuesday to realize that in addition to screwing up with the whole Calvin and Osito situation, I'd also screwed up my coding project. I'd planned to use footage of Osito in the video, maybe coax him into barking, and then add my voice-over so it looked like part of the video was a cute dog talking. But with all the craziness last week, I'd never gotten the footage.

I went over to Phoebe's after school on Tuesday, and she set up her camera and I tried to read my script, but I kept messing up. My heart just wasn't in it.

"You do remember that the project is due on *Monday*, right?" Phoebe asked me after I'd messed up yet another take. "And you said yourself you're not going to have much of a weekend, with the quince happening and all your relatives in town."

"I know!" I wailed, and threw myself down onto Phoebe's bed.

Phoebe stared at me. "Never thought I'd see the day. Ana Ramos. Procrastinating."

"I'm not doing it on purpose. It's just so hard to focus. Every time I try, I flash back to Calvin's face when I told him. He was so mad."

"So you've mentioned nineteen or a thousand times," Phoebe

said. "But come on. Just read the script, I'll film you, and we'll knock this out. Your coding will be amazing, I'm sure. You'll get a pretty good grade no matter what."

Part of me knew Phoebe was right, but part of me was afraid that just a "pretty good grade" might cost me the top slot. It was late April—not too many more chances to bring grades up.

I took a deep breath and followed Phoebe's advice. I read the script straight through without messing up.

Phoebe played part of the video back to check the recording. My voice sounded flat, like I didn't care about Waggle Walkers, or even much of anything at all.

"You've got to shake this off," Phoebe said. "Calvin will forgive you. And if not, he wasn't really your friend to begin with."

"But he was a great friend. I was the bad friend."

"Ana, it'll be okay. I promise."

I stood up. "I know you're right. It's just kind of an overwhelming week, with the quince, like you said."

Neither of us said what we both knew I was thinking: I no longer had an escort to the quince.

Calvin had stopped speaking to me at school. When we passed in the hall he'd always be talking to somebody else so he didn't even need to meet my eyes.

Of course I knew I could try to find another escort at the last minute, but I couldn't bring myself to look. I'd go alone and face the embarrassment. Besides, I figured it was probably what I deserved.

When I got back from Phoebe's, I saw what looked like a moving truck in front of our building. I did a double take. A man was lowering the big metal grate at the back of the truck, and before I got close enough see who else might be inside, the truck had pulled away from the curb and out into traffic.

I ran into the building and up the stairs to the fifth floor.

I knew I'd been right when I saw that the door to Mrs. R's place was standing open. I walked forward slowly, knowing I was about to see an empty apartment.

I looked inside—it was completely empty. Our building's super, Mr. Martin, came up behind me.

"Excuse me," he said, walking around me. "Oh, hello, Ana.

If you're looking for Mrs. Ramirez, you definitely missed her." He added the last part with a chuckle.

"Did she just leave?" I asked.

"No, she hasn't been back since she went to the hospital—her daughter sent a moving company here. It took them all day to pack up her things and get the place cleared out."

"So is she going to be living with her daughter in Baltimore now?" I asked, afraid of the answer.

"I'm afraid I don't know. But that would make sense. I know she's been struggling living in a walk-up. I'm sure this is for the best."

"I'm sure it is. Thanks, Mr. Martin," I told him.

I walked with heavy steps back down to the fourth floor.

Mrs. Ramirez—and Osito—seemed to be gone for good.

Even if it was for the best, I didn't want to accept it. The thought of never seeing Osito again felt like someone had punched a hole in my heart.

Maybe Mom was right and it was better never to even have a pet, if this was what losing one felt like.

20

Hope

The garden outside our community center looked magical. The many twinkle lights Mom had ordered were strung up everywhere, and they sparkled against the evening sky. I heard the strains of the band's music coming from inside the building.

After so much preparation, it was hard to believe that the day was finally here: Tali's *quinceañera*.

It was also still so hard to believe how badly I'd messed everything up.

The thing was, once I'd asked Calvin to go to Tali's quince,

I'd actually almost started to look forward to it. But now there was no Calvin.

I looked down at myself in the Ruffle Monster. The dress reminded me of Calvin, too—of the day we'd searched for Pancake and I'd missed out on shopping with Mom.

I stood there, alone, as guests walked past me and into the community center. My parents and Tali had arrived earlier to set things up, but I'd made up an excuse about having to finish some homework so I could lag behind and come on my own. Thankfully, my parents were so frantic that they agreed to this plan. Now I could no longer avoid the inevitable.

It *was* true that I still had to finish my coding project. But I wasn't able to focus on it today, not with relatives constantly calling. My plan was to tackle the project tomorrow so I'd be prepared to present it on Monday. I'd try my best to get an A and keep my grade point average where it was. At this point I figured it was all I could do.

I stepped inside the lobby, which was crowded with guests— friends and classmates of Tali's, tons of family members (including Cousin Javier, who was showing off his karate moves to some other cousins), and, of course, Tali herself. She stood there beaming beside her escort, Alex, who looked really handsome in his tux. Tali was a vision in her pink dress, which fit perfectly now. My eyes filled with tears at how pretty and happy my sister looked. As crazy as everything had been, she deserved to have her big day go well.

A bunch of the littlest kids were gathering in the corner, whooping, and I saw what had drawn their attention: The big pink piñata was hanging there. The one that Calvin had bought.

Calvin, again.

At that moment it was all too much. The happy tears that had gathered at the sight of Tali were threatening to turn into something else.

I knew the party was going to start soon, but I needed another moment alone. I hurried through the crowd and ran back outside.

And that's when I saw him, standing under the twinkle lights in a tuxedo.

Calvin.

I stared at him, then blinked in case I'd imagined him there. I took a step closer. He was really here. He looked older than he did in his everyday clothes.

"Calvin . . . what are you doing . . . I thought . . . ?" I stumbled over my words and gave up, still staring at him in surprise.

"Hey, Ana," he said quietly, giving me a half smile. "Look, this doesn't mean that I'm okay with . . . that I completely forgive you for . . . everything. But I didn't want you to have to come to this alone. I know how much you were dreading it."

I swiped at my eyes, starting to smile, too. "I was. That was really . . . nice of you. I . . . it would be awkward to be without an escort, since it's my sister's quince."

Calvin's face changed. "Oh. If you found another escort, I'll go . . . I should have asked." He took a step backward.

"No! I mean, I didn't. Find another escort. I'm alone."

Calvin's expression softened. "Not anymore. So . . . that's the Ruffle Monster, huh?" He gestured to my dress.

I felt myself blush. I'd forgotten that I'd told him my nickname for the dress.

"Yeah. It's horrible, I know."

"It's not so bad. But I know you hate it, so I apologize."

"Wait, why would you apologize?"

"Phoebe told me. About how your mom got the dress for you after you were late. When you were finding Pancake."

I shook my head. "I'd wear this every day if it meant making sure Pancake was safe."

"She told me you said that, too," Calvin said.

He was staring at me, but not like he was angry. I couldn't figure out the expression on his face.

Just then, Mom stuck her head outside. "It's time to line up for your part, Ana," she told me.

"Okay," I told her. "Oh, this is my escort. This is Calvin. Calvin, this is my mom."

"Hi, Mrs. Ramos," Calvin said. I thought again how grown-up he seemed, in his tux, with his perfect manners.

Even Mom wasn't immune to Calvin's charm, and she gave him a big smile. Then she looked over at me. There was a question in her eyes, but I knew she wouldn't say anything now. She just gestured for me and Calvin to follow her inside.

"So will you warn me if I have to do anything specific?" Calvin asked me as we stepped back inside and walked through the lobby.

"Tali has fourteen sets of attendants, one for each year of her life," I explained. "I'm—well, we're—two of them. We have to walk in when they call us, and then stand there."

"Okay, cool," Calvin said. "I can do that."

We walked together into the big empty space at the Loisaida Center. Tali and I had taken dance and theater lessons there when we were younger. It was strange to see the space now transformed for a formal party. On one side of the room was the huge table that was already full of food. I heard my stomach rumble— we'd just had cold sandwiches as an early lunch, and I couldn't wait until the ceremonial part was over and we could eat.

Tali stood on the stage with her escort, still looking beautiful and surprisingly calm. The band stopped playing and my father stepped up on the stage, using the microphone to call for all the *damas* and their escorts to line up.

"This is our moment," I whispered to Calvin.

He offered me his arm and I took it, feeling a little flutter of nerves in my belly. For the first time it hit me just how embarrassing this part would have been without him here. I would have survived it, of course, but sometimes you want to do more than just survive stuff.

We all lined up by age, with Calvin and me at the back of the line. I could see Tali's friends Ella and Haley with their escorts up front. The band started playing an instrumental version of one of Tali's favorite songs, and we all walked through the middle of the big room, between two rows of chairs that had been set up. Papi announced everyone's names, and we stepped forward and faced the crowd, forming a semicircle on two sides in front of the band's platform. We were leaving space for Tali, who walked in last with Alex. Papi introduced Tali, getting a little teary-eyed as he said, "Today my little girl is becoming a woman."

He handed the microphone to Tali. I heard just a little quiver of nerves in her voice. I already knew her speech by heart, since she'd been practicing it out loud in our room for weeks. First, she thanked our parents for taking care of her and supporting her, and for throwing her this party. Then she thanked me for being a great sister. Calvin turned to me and I smiled, my face flushed.

"While I'm on the subject of my sister, Ana, could you come up here?" Tali asked. "I have something for you."

I started walking toward the stage while Tali kept talking.

"I'm cheating a little bit here," Tali explained to the crowd in her charming way. "My friend Bianca's family is from Mexico, and she gave her sister a doll on her quince day. That got me thinking about *my* sister. So I'm borrowing that tradition, but putting my own spin on it."

I climbed the stairs of the stage and faced Tali.

"My sister, Ana, isn't much of a doll person," Tali went on. "She gave them up a long time ago, as a matter of fact. But I do have a special 'doll' for my very special sister." She handed me a big box wrapped in—of course—shiny pink paper. I ripped the paper off and laughed when I saw what was inside. It was a kit to build your own solar-powered robot. Perfect for me.

I held up the doll/robot to show everyone. Most people cheered, though I noticed my great-aunt looked pretty confused.

Then it was time for the dancing. Tali and her escort, Alex, started off, and then all of the *damas* with their escorts were supposed to join in. I felt a sudden rush of nervousness at the thought of dancing with Calvin.

I'd known for a long time that I'd have to dance—that this part of the quince party would call for it. But when Calvin had stopped talking to me, I'd expected to sit out this part.

Nothing could have prepared me for the way it felt when Calvin, looking so handsome in his tuxedo, reached for my hand. Even though he'd said that coming tonight didn't really change anything, I couldn't help but feel a swell of hope that maybe it would.

The band was playing a song that sounded familiar. Knowing Tali, it had been in some romantic movie she'd made me watch. I followed Calvin the few steps it took to reach an open spot in the small area reserved for dancing. Calvin put one hand on my waist, and I darted a look over at Tali to remind myself what I was supposed to do. I'd danced at other quince parties before, but it had always been with one of my cousins or a family friend. Calvin seemed to know what he was doing, though.

"You're good at this. Dancing," I told him, looking up at him for the first time.

"My mom's job again," he said. "Remember, this is my tux. Most of the events I've had to wear it to, I've also had to know how to dance."

"Did you take lessons?"

He laughed, and we were so close I could feel the rumble in his chest. "No, my sister taught me."

"That doesn't sound so bad."

"Well, Chelsea kept making fun of me for stepping on her feet."

"Ah, that might make it less fun," I agreed. "My older sister never makes fun of me. My cousin Javier is the one who does that," I added, nodding to where Javier was dancing in the corner with his mom.

"That was cool how your sister gave you a robot."

"Yeah, she likes to put her own spin on things for sure."

Calvin grinned. "Speaking of spins . . ."

Calvin spun me around in an expert way. I felt a laugh bubble up out of my chest. I'd dreaded this night for so long, and now here I was, dancing and laughing. With Calvin. And for the moment, it seemed we'd both forgotten about the Osito lie.

I realized then that the song had ended and everyone was leaving the dance floor. The official part of the dancing was over. Calvin said he was going to the bathroom and I pointed out to him where it was.

The minute he left my side, Tali appeared, grabbing my elbow.

"Calvin came!"

"Shh!" I said, pulling her farther away, to the other side of the room. "Yes, he showed up. He said he didn't want me to have to come alone," I added once we were in a slightly more private spot. I glanced around. "Don't you have more important things to attend to, birthday girl?" I asked.

My sister's eyes sparkled. "My guests can wait. So he just showed up? You didn't know he was coming? That's so romantic!"

I shook my head. "He still hasn't forgiven me for lying. He just came tonight to help me out. That's all."

"Uh-huh," Tali said, in a tone that meant she didn't believe him at all. "Come on, let's get some punch for your *escort* while we're over here."

"Okay," I said. The truth was I hoped more than anything that Tali was right. But I'd already had my heart broken once this week when I lost Osito. Hoping for something, I knew, didn't always work out.

The rest of the evening seemed to fly by. Papi presented Tali with the traditional pair of high-heeled shoes to symbolize her growing up. But since our mom was our mom, the heels were still pretty low. I caught Tali's eye and winked at her as she stood up in them. Then we all feasted on delicious food: chicken and rice, roast pork, *arroz con gandules*, *blanditas*, all kinds of salads, flan, and a big white cake. Calvin ate every bite off his plate, even trying the more unfamiliar foods—well, at least the ones that were vegetarian. I was impressed. And again, so grateful to have him there.

Before I knew it, someone turned on the overhead lights, and it was time to go home.

"Thank you for coming," I told Calvin as I walked him outside. I'd have to stay later to help my family pack up and bring all the presents and leftover food home. "This would have been . . . really embarrassing without an escort. After everything, you still coming . . . I just . . . thank you."

"You're welcome," Calvin said, his hands in his pockets. He'd seemed open and relaxed all night, but now he seemed stiff again, clearly remembering Osito. "I . . . I had a nice time."

"Me, too," I said.

Calvin checked his cell phone. "Okay, my dad's coming to get me, so I should go. I'll see you at school."

I looked down at my feet. The Calvin who'd spun me on the dance floor seemed to have vanished. My hopes sank, and my heart felt tight in my chest.

"See you at school," I echoed. But when I looked up, he was already gone.

21

You've Got Everything
You Need

I went over to Phoebe's on Sunday afternoon to finally finish up my coding project. First, I filled her in on the *quinceañera* and how Calvin had shown up. She was excited, and wanted to discuss it at length, but I told her I didn't really feel like talking about it. And I needed to focus on schoolwork now—specifically, the presentation for Waggle Walkers.

"I have some stock images I saved," I explained, opening my laptop on Phoebe's bed, "and of course the footage you shot. I was hoping you could shape it into *something*, at least."

"Move over, let me drive," Phoebe said, shooing me away from my laptop. "Hey, what's in this folder?"

"What are you doing?" I reached for the computer. "That's just stuff Calvin's sent me. Like pug pictures, and memes and stuff." Trust my BFF to go opening all the random files on my computer.

Phoebe clicked on the folder. "Some of these are of Osito. And Pancake. You acted like you never got any footage of them!"

"I *meant* to film Osito barking, to make it look like he was talking," I explained. "But in all the chaos I just never got around to it."

"Ana, I know it was my idea and all, but I'm no longer convinced that the whole talking dog concept is the only way to go here," Phoebe told me.

"Then why didn't you say . . . ?"

"You got so stuck on it that I never said anything. But you've got all kinds of great stuff here—in fact, you've got everything you need. Let's just record one more voice-over about how you took care of Osito—add that personal touch—and I'll put it all together."

"Are you serious? You think you can use some of this and make it okay?"

"Who are you talking to?" Phoebe asked with a snort. "I'll make it *awesome*."

The plan was, we were supposed to email Ms. V our websites on Monday morning, so she would have time to evaluate them before our class presentations. The grades we got would be based mainly on the sites, but our presentations counted, too.

In coding class that afternoon, Calvin went first. His presentation for his New York newbies website was great, but I could see that his site was pretty basic. I had planned to help him with the coding, I remembered then. Until he had, very justifiably, stopped talking to me. I sighed.

When he was finished, he sat down beside me, looking a little disappointed. For the first time, though, I wasn't thinking about grades and how I had to be the top in the class.

"That was good," I told Calvin, wanting to be supportive.

"Thanks," he whispered to me, but he was focused on the next presentation.

I had trouble paying attention because I was getting really nervous for my presentation. But I did cheer for Phoebe when she presented her great filmmaking website. And then, finally, it was my turn.

I stood up and handed Ms. Vasquez my laptop so she could cue up my video presentation. She had a printout of my Waggle Walkers site in front of her, to refer to as I spoke. She nodded at me.

"My website is called Waggle Walkers," I began.

I stood in front of the class, knowing that Calvin was watching. I concentrated on the presentation that came up on screen—with Phoebe's help, it had really come out well. There were images of Osito and Pancake. Two doggy best friends. And lots of other funny dog memes from the folder on my laptop. There was also voice-over: me talking about how much dogs bring to our lives. Phoebe had sneak-recorded me; she'd gotten me talking about why I loved dogs so much and recorded me without my knowing. When I was so upset that every time I tried to read my script I sounded like a robot, Phoebe had found a way to get me to loosen up. She was right, I realized. All along, for my project, I'd had everything I needed. All the footage from Calvin, and the two pugs—and my amazing best friend to put all the pieces together.

When the video was over, everyone clapped, which surprised me. Ms. V looked extra proud. I gave Phoebe a grateful look and mouthed *Thank you.* Then I finally met Calvin's eye. He gave me a small smile and then a thumbs-up sign. I told myself not to take the gesture too seriously, remembering how cold he'd seemed at the end of the quince. It was dangerous to hope too much, I reminded myself.

At the end of class, Ms. V handed us back printouts of our sites with our grades on them. I looked down and my stomach jumped when I saw my grade: *A.* I was relieved and happy. But I had other things on my mind, too.

At lunch the next day, Phoebe waved Calvin over to our table.

"How'd you do on your coding project?" she asked him. "I got a B-plus."

"Same here," Calvin said.

I looked down at my cup of soup. What I'd wanted had come

true—I'd gotten a higher grade than Calvin, which meant that I likely still had the top spot in the grade, and would likely get the Crown Point Prize. I was excited, and proud of myself for my hard work. But suddenly, the idea of winning—of everything going according to plan—no longer seemed as important as it once had.

I realized Calvin was talking to me. "Your website was great, Ana," he was saying. "I could see how it would really help people who need dog walkers. Like, um, your neighbor," he added.

Suddenly everything felt awkward again. My cheeks flamed in embarrassment.

Why, oh, why hadn't I trusted Calvin enough to tell him the truth? After all, he'd never been anything but helpful and nice, since that first day in the park when he'd carried my bag and helped me get out of the pounding rain.

Phoebe jumped in to fill the silence. "I think we *all* did great work."

"Thanks," Calvin said. "Well, I gotta go. Bye, you guys."

I sighed as he walked away.

"You've still got it bad," Phoebe said.

I gave a start and dropped the spoon I'd been holding in midair—probably for an awkwardly long time, now that I thought about it. "What? I don't . . . I mean, I'm not . . ."

Phoebe snorted. "You've got just as big a crush on him as ever. The question is, what are you going to do about it?"

"I'm not going to do anything right now. He's still not over my lying to him. He said . . ."

Phoebe made a dismissive noise. "You gotta strike while the iron's still hot. Do you want to wait until Lucy Alvarez gets her hooks into him?"

"Low blow."

"Just trying to help you out, my friend. Besides, what do you have to lose? What's the worst that can happen? If he says he still can't forgive you—well, then, at least you'll know. But the worst thing that can happen if you do nothing? Well. Calvin's a cute and nice guy. If it's not Lucy, somebody else will notice that before too long."

Phoebe was right, as usual. It was finally time to admit that I did like Calvin—a lot. And it was time for me to be brave.

"Okay. Say I do want to do something. How do I show him I'm sorry—and that I've changed?" I asked.

"I don't know exactly. But whatever it is, I think it should be big. You kind of messed up big time. In the movies, it always takes a grand gesture to apologize for something like that."

"A grand gesture, huh? Like what?"

"Play to your strengths," Phoebe advised sagely, while trying without much success to punch a hole in her Capri Sun pack.

Just like that, I had an idea. I stood up and picked up my lunch bag. "I have to go. I'm going to get started right now."

"Wait!" Phoebe called.

I stepped back. "What is it?"

She raised her drink packet and the straw. "Open this first?"

I laughed, punched in the straw, and headed to the library to get started on my idea.

WEBSITE ~~DESIGN IDEAS~~ PLAN

Website name: Calvin's NYC

Place ideas:

–BEST smoothies—at Succo.

–Historical sites downtown: Federal Hall, Tenement Museum, Trinity Church, maybe Custom House?

–Meatless Mexican—best veggie enchiladas since he likes Mexican food and doesn't eat meat.

–Final stop: Tyro's Bike Shop.

22

Calvin's NYC

I took a deep breath and composed the text. First, I copied in the URL of the website I'd made for Calvin. Then I wrote my apology:

Calvin, I'm so sorry I lied to you and didn't trust you. It wasn't fair.

I made this for you. I know you're not too sure about NYC, and that you miss Florida. But there's so much in my hometown for you to love. I thought maybe I could show some of it to you.

This website will take you to some places that I hope you will like.

If you decide to do this tour, it needs to start on Sunday morning at nine. There will be a surprise for you at each stop if you do.

Hope you can make it!

Ana

Then I held my breath, and hit send.

An hour later, I got a text back.

Wow, a whole website 4 me? Ok—I'll start the hunt @9 on Sunday ☺

A smiley face seemed like a good sign! I sent back a ☺ of my own and got back to planning.

All day Saturday was devoted to running around getting everything set up for Calvin's scavenger hunt. The website would give him directions to each spot and a hint about what he would find there. I enlisted Phoebe and Tali, of course, and my sister got Ella and Haley to help, too.

The plan was this: I was sending Calvin to five stops. Tali was the first stop—she would meet Calvin at the gift shop at the Tenement Museum. She would give him a book on the history of the Lower East Side. Next, Ella and Haley would meet him at Succo and give him a green smoothie.

I really wanted to add another historical stop, but nothing was open on Sunday. Phoebe convinced me that what I had planned would be cool enough, so next I was sending him to Meatless Mexican, where Phoebe would be waiting with a to-go order of veggie enchiladas.

The final stop would be Tyro's Bike Shop.

I was really hoping that part would go well.

Thanks to helping Mrs. Ramirez with Osito for a year, I had a bunch of money saved. I wasn't much of a spender. I wasn't even really sure what I'd been saving up for. I'd wanted a robot kit for a while, but Tali had gotten me that for her quince.

So I used all the Osito money to get Calvin a bike. With the help of the kind people at the shop, I'd picked out a few options and paid enough to cover whichever one he would choose. Tali would meet Calvin there to tell him he should pick out the brand and color and style he wanted.

And then the final stop was me. If Calvin wanted to, he could come see me at the park where we met. If he didn't, I told myself, that was okay, too. At least I'd know that I had tried.

23

Completely Perfect

On Sunday, I got up bright and early and texted all my helpers to make sure the plan was in place. It was. When Tali texted me that Calvin had shown up at the Tenement Museum, I knew he was following my hints and the route. That made me excited. So excited I couldn't focus on the homework I had planned to do that day.

I decided to go for a walk to get rid of some of my pent-up energy. I walked over to the deli and got a bagel with cream cheese. On my way back home, it started to rain—a fast, heavy shower—a lot like the day I'd met Calvin, but without the lightning and thunder. I hadn't brought an umbrella, so I got soaked in minutes.

Shivering, I raced for my building. My first thought was that I hoped the rain wouldn't stop Calvin from finishing the route.

My second was that, if by some miracle he actually wanted to come see me at the end, I now looked like a drowned rat.

I hurried up the stairs to our apartment and unlocked our front door. I heard familiar voices in the living room; my parents were in there, speaking with a woman. But who?

And then, before I could even step all the way inside—I saw him. A tiny, adorable, black pug barreling toward me at top speed, tongue and tail wagging.

Osito!

"Osito!" I cried. I couldn't believe it was really him.

When he reached me, he pawed frantically at my legs, asking to be picked up. I scooped him up and gave him a kiss on his soft, furry cheek. Oh, how I'd missed my little bear!

I finally walked into the living room, Osito in my arms, and realized that it was Rosa who sat there talking to my parents.

"Hello, Ana!" she said with a smile.

"Hi, Rosa. How is your mom feeling?" I asked as Osito licked my cheek. I laughed.

"She's doing a little better, thank you. And I wanted to thank you again for doing such a fine job cleaning her apartment."

"Oh, it's not a big deal," I said, sitting down with Osito on my lap. "I was glad to help."

Rosa looked expectantly at my parents, as though she was waiting for them to say something. I looked from my mom to my dad, confused.

"Ana, Rosa came here to tell us that Mrs. Ramirez has decided that it's too much for her, caring for Osito," Mom finally said.

My heart started pounding, and without thinking I held Osito tighter against me. That was why Rosa had come, then. To let me say a final good-bye.

I felt Osito's soft fur against my face, hugged his warm, wriggly little body, and tried not to cry.

"So who is adopting him?" I managed to ask, though my throat felt almost too tight to speak.

"I would have kept him, for my mom," Rosa said. "But my

son doesn't do well with him. It's just a little too much for us right now."

I looked up at Rosa; I didn't understand what she was saying.

Papi cleared his throat and spoke. "Rosa has come today, Ana, to see if *you* would be interested in adopting Osito."

I felt my mouth drop open.

"Me? But I'm not allowed . . ."

Mom shook her head. "Your father and I have had a discussion. We've both noticed how much you've grown up recently. You've taken on more chores around the house. You really rose to the occasion for your sister's quince. And you've always been caring—the way you helped Mrs. Ramirez all this time shows that. Your father pointed out that those are the qualities of a good pet owner."

"But—but you don't like animals," I sputtered.

Mom gave a small smile. "I've never been much of a dog or cat person, it's true. Your *abuelita* didn't allow us to have any pets, you know. But just like your father and I have seen with you . . . people can change."

I sat staring at my mom. It sounded like she was saying . . . but I still couldn't quite believe it. I just needed her to say the actual words.

"So what we're saying is, if you would like to keep Osito, and if you promise to be a responsible pet owner, we will allow it," Mom said.

That's when I really did start crying, but they were definitely happy tears. I hugged Osito close to me and cried on his fur, and then I set him down and hugged Mom, and Papi, and then Rosa.

Then everyone started laughing, me included, and Osito danced around happily, confused at the noise but picking up on our joy.

My phone buzzed in my pocket. I pulled it out and read the message from Tali. I blinked and read it again. It couldn't be. Two pieces of amazing news in one day?

"He's coming to the park!" I yelled.

"I'm glad Calvin forgives you," Mom said with a wink.

"Wait, how did you . . ." I gave a sigh as I realized. "Tali."

"Did you forget that your sister is the worst secret keeper in the world?" Papi asked with a chuckle.

I shook my head, but I couldn't get mad at Tali, because I was too busy grinning at her message. And down at Osito. "I'm so sorry, Rosa—I don't want to rush off . . ."

She waved a hand. "I have to go soon anyway, Ana. I'm so glad that you and Osito will be together. I know you will take such good care of him—and give him all the exercise that Mom couldn't. She did ask if you would promise to send her pictures and updates, though."

"Of course!" I said. "I can't thank you enough for bringing him to me," I added, more tears springing to my eyes.

Rosa hugged me one more time, and then Mom and Papi told me I could go ahead. And since Osito was now—really and truly—*mine* (!), I could take him along.

I got my little bear into his halter with fingers that were still trembling with excitement. Then I waved good-bye to my parents and Rosa, scooped up Osito, and went downstairs. I walked quickly toward the park. It wasn't until I passed by a parked car that I remembered about getting caught in the rain. My hair was mostly dry now, but in the reflection it looked all frizzy and wild. With my free hand, I smoothed my hair down the best I could. Oh well; I wasn't going to risk missing Calvin at the park to go back upstairs to fix it.

The rest of the walk to the park seemed to take forever, like I was walking through Jell-O or something. I didn't know what I was going to say to Calvin—or what he would say to me—I just wanted to get there.

Finally, I reached the gates to the dog run. I looked inside, but didn't see Calvin anywhere. A wave of disappointment crashed over me. What if I missed him? Or what if he'd told Tali he was coming, but then he didn't?

But then I saw him, riding toward me on his new bike. On the front of the bike I saw he'd added a basket—and inside sat Pancake!

Calvin came to a stop beside me. "I hope you don't mind—I went home to get Pancake."

"Of course not!" I said. "I like the basket. Great addition."

"Well, I knew you'd want one for Osito," he said with a grin as he stepped off the bike.

"Wait—what?"

Calvin picked up Pancake and sat her on the ground. "Don't worry, I got a basket on mine for her, too."

"On *yours*—but this is yours. Didn't Tali explain . . . ?"

Calvin stepped closer to me. "Your sister explained everything. She told me about you getting me a bike . . . and she told me about how your parents were going to let you adopt Osito."

Tali again! Trust my sister to know everything before I did.

"Yes, I get to keep him!" I exclaimed. "He's *really* mine this time. And I'm so sorry I lied . . ."

"Ana, you don't have to say anything else. I've had some time to think about all of it. I understand now why you didn't tell me. I wish you'd trusted me, but I also see now that your parents are different from mine—stricter, maybe. Phoebe pointed out that you were worried that my parents would say no, if it were only your neighbor's dog."

I smiled at my best friend's wonderful meddling. "I really am sorry."

"I know. Let's just make a promise that, from now on, we'll always tell the truth. Deal?"

"Deal," I agreed. "But, Calvin, I don't understand what you meant about the bike. I remember you saying that you were saving up for a bike, so I know you wanted one."

Calvin grinned. "I did say that. You're a good listener. But, Ana—I've been paying in installments for my own bike at a place my dad found. I actually paid it off last week. So, I picked this bike for *you* instead today. You can't let me go biking around this big city all alone, can you? I mean, I saw a lot of cool things today, but there's so much more to see. I think I still need a local to show me around . . ."

Calvin didn't get to say anything else then because, without stopping to think, I stood up on my tiptoes and gave him a kiss.

My first kiss.

He looked a little bit surprised when I pulled away, but he was smiling.

"I can't believe you were going to buy me a bike," he told me. He moved my hair off my face and I no longer cared that it looked wild. I realized Calvin didn't care, either. In fact, his expression seemed to say that he liked my hair the way it was. My heart jumped.

"I can't believe I kissed you," I blurted out.

Calvin grinned. "I'm glad you did," he said. He put a hand on my waist and pulled me even closer to him, and then he kissed me again.

"So do you like the bike I picked for you?" he asked.

I nodded, still feeling a little breathless from both kisses. "I do. Green's my favorite color."

"I figured. You wear a lot of green." *Calvin had noticed what I wore?* I grinned up at him, feeling like I was in a dream. First, I got to keep my sweet Osito, forever. And now Calvin was here, giving *me* a bike, and kissing me. Everything was absolutely, completely perfect.

"My bike's at home," Calvin said. "Want to come pick it up with me, and then we can go for a ride with the pugs?" he asked.

"Yes," I said. "That's exactly what I want to do."

Acknowledgments

Suzie Townsend and Sara Stricker—you guys rock—thank you for always helping me navigate the writing world!

Danielle Barthel, thank you for all your help on this and lots of other projects—can't wait to hear about your new adventures.

Aimee Friedman, thank you for all the editing magic—you make it look easy.

Thank you Sara Cintrón-Schultz for your invaluable insight into Ana's world.

A special shout-out to Gabriella—for so much reading and revising feedback. Miss our period 2s in the café already.

Thank you, Heather (aka Story Wizard) for helping me come up with so many ideas. Pancake couldn't have gotten lost and found without you.

Thank you, Mandy, for helping me figure out 2017—and letting me pick Giovanni's almost all the time even though you usually wanted to go to Toasted.

Sarah, thank you for the amazing opportunity for a new life this year—can't wait to share this story, and lots of others, with my new school family.

Thank you to my wonderful mom for always being there.

As always, thank you to my best friend Nikki for always, always listening. And to my wonderful chicas (and the man)—thanks for being my friends.

Finally, for all my students (but this year especially, my class of 2019)—you guys make it all worthwhile. Keep on reading!

Can't get enough of puppy love?

Be sure to read: